Terror at
Visitation Lake

By

W. A. Holmes

For information, or to order additional copies,
please contact:

Beacon Publishing Group
P.O. Box 41573 Charleston, S.C. 29423
800.817.8480| beaconpublishinggroup.com

Publisher's catalog available by request.

ISBN-13: 978-1-949472-19-6

ISBN-10: 1-949472-19-6

Published in 2020. New York, NY 10001.

First Edition. Printed in the USA.

Dedicated to my wife, Gail, of 40 years, and our seven children: Rachel, Nate, Rebekah, Jesse, Tim, Luke, and Anna.

Chapter 1

Justin Alastair Thyme unconsciously rubbed the small scar under his chin. His left hand cradled a wide-angle lens. It was tough to decide: use the new zoom lens, or the wide angle?

GenEx Labs swarmed with media representatives scrambling to set up equipment in preparation for a live broadcast. In just a few hours, GenEx would receive a major donation from Dr. Louis Siffer, and Justin's father—physician and senior biomedical engineer at GenEx—would be on hand to accept the donation.

Justin's purpose in life was to capture everything on film. At home, a police scanner sat on the night table next to his bed and kept him up-to-date on all the current action in Angel Falls.

He chose the zoom lens. The enormity of the GenEx Labs reception area made it his best choice.

All he needed to do was align the red dot on the lens with the red dot on the camera body with a twist and *click* and the Minolta X-700 was ready. He'd saved for two months to buy the second-hand camera. He'd bought the lens six weeks later.

Tall and slender, Justin little resembled the stocky scientist he called dad. This was nto a surprise, since Mark and Jean Thyme had adopted him as an infant. Other than the small scar on his chin, the sandy-haired teen had no other distinguishing features, except that he towered over his relatives. Everyone at family gatherings looked up to Justin—literally.

Angel Falls, where GenEx Labs was located, was a midwestern town with a population of just under one hundred eighty thousand. It had been Justin's home for as long as he could remember. With the help of his police scanner he remained in the middle of whatever excitement the town had to offer.

Of course, when he wanted an escape from too much acitivity, he turned to the tranquility of Visitation Lake. It was his favorite secluded spot, situated high above the town on the plateau fifteen miles to the west. It was also the best place to take nature photos.

Justin panned the room through the viewfinder, before everything went black. He looked up to see a rotund figure standing over him. "Your dad must have some clout to get them to allow you in here," the figure said. It was Mike Gordon, the head of security.

"Hey, Mike. Keeping the place safe from terrorists?" Justin asked playfully.

Mike half smiled as he wiped his forehead with his coat sleeve. "Trying to keep cool. These extra people put a strain on the air con."

"Losing a few pounds might help too."

"Does your dad know what a troublemaker you are?" Mike shot back, wiping his forehead with his sleeve again. "You'd better not pull anything. Get that stuffy Siffer in a tizzy and he'll take his money someplace else."

Justin laughed. "You don't like him much, do you?"

"Him and his donations! Ever since he reorganized the place he's been throwing his weight around like some big shot."

"You've got the weight around here, Mike," Justin said with a grin. "Besides, you sort of owe your job to the good doctor."

"Yeah, right. Then he goes around like some celebrity making me work twice as hard to keep an eye on things."

"So you actually have to do some work." Justin playfully provoked Mike whenever he could. But he knew celebrities made security more difficult. There was crowd control to consider. When everyone's attention gets diverted to the special guest, it leaves an opening for corporate espionage or other funny business.

Mike changed the subject. "That's a nice lens. New?"

"Like it? Here, take a look." Justin handed him the camera.

Mike scanned the huge arena, zooming in and out as he turned around. Still looking through the viewfinder, he said, "I never see you without that ratty camera bag of yours. Isn't it time to replace it?"

"I'd rather spend the money on lenses. Besides, nobody would steal that old thing, so my stuff is safe inside."

"Subterfuge. Just the kind of stuff I need to be on the lookout for," Mike said, and then he stopped short. "Better go. Looks like I may be needed." He quickly handed the camera back to Justin.

"Be gentle!" Justin called as Mike disappeared into the crowd.

Like a den of snakes, cables of all kinds had been laid across the GenEx lobby, running in and out of control booths and equipment. This major multimedia event attracted all the national and local networks. Two major newspapers, one from the East Coast and one from the West, as well as Angel Falls' own Tribune, were also present. Several science journals were on hand, with reporters and analysts setting up recording equipment.

Justin looked several yards to his left where one of the reporters questioned his dad.

"Sir, your name is spelled T-H-Y-M-E and pronounced 'Time', right?"

4

"Just like the seasoning, that's right." Mark smiled and winked at his son.

GenEx Labs was the town's largest employer, famous for its work in genetic research and biotechnology. They had recently perfected a method to save premature babies using nanotechnology. Microscopic robots had been engineered to produce and carry oxygen to programmed destinations, primarily the vital organs of the body. It gave these babies the edge they needed to survive. What the preemie's underdeveloped lungs could not do, the nanobots did. Justin's dad was primarily responsible for developing this technology.

His father now worked on preliminary experimentation aimed at using nanobots to stimulate damaged nerves with electrical impulses. The results had been very promising. The primary application, repair of spinal injuries, had the potential to restore lost movement in the arms and legs.

Justin got several shots of the interior of the building. The opportunity to get inside GenEx did not come often, but when it did, Justin made sure he caught its distinctive architecture on film. The circular reception lobby was large enough to swallow an entire football field. A permit was required to bring a camera inside any of the buildings. The lobby was the only area with no photo restrictions.

Justin decided to brave the central, spiral staircase to the second floor walkway. He flung the camera bag over his shoulder and secured the strap around his neck. Then he gripped the camera tightly with one hand, the wrought iron handrail with the other, and began to walk upstairs.

Halfway to the second floor he paused, feeling flush. He took several deep breaths, careful not to look up or down, but straight across and out past the structure's three-story glass window. Beyond it, the waters of Falls River churned rapidly. Now he was getting light-headed.

Just a few more steps and he would make it to the second floor walkway. From there, it got tricky. High above the lobby, the walkway extended north to south through the center of the rotunda. Each end connected to the central balcony, a circular second floor hallway with access to the rest of the one-hundred-forty-acre complex.

Getting some shots from there would be like winning a medal. He'd tried using the elevator but never made it to the center of the walkway. Even if he could conquer the stairs, he still had the walkway to deal with.

But height wasn't Justin's only issue with the walkway. It was transparent, with only a four-foot high glass partition running the length of each side for protection. Standing in the middle gave the sensation of being suspended in mid-air.

"Just a bit further," he coaxed himself out loud.

One more step and he pulled himself up onto clear nothingness. Beads of perspiration began to form on his slick forehead and trickle down his temples. "Come on!" he urged angrily.

Holding on to the partition for dear life, he forced himself to look only at the trees beyond the river. Then he fumbled for his camera with one hand and put the viewfinder to his eye. He inhaled slowly, held his breath, and looked down at lobby through the viewfinder. Observing everything close-up through the lens seemed to make the climb less threatening. He snapped the shutter.

Encouraged, he kept the camera up to his eye, maintained a tight grip on the rail, and continued to scan the reception area below. He took as many shots as he could, feeling relieved that he had remembered to install the automatic film winder earlier that day.

Normally fifty employees manned the central reception console, including security guards and other personnel. They controlled all traffic in and out of GenEx. The area was busier today than Justin had ever seen it, all because of Doctor Siffer, their special guest.

Behind and to the sides of the console were several banks of elevators. Justin wasn't the only person who hated the stairway. Very tight security slowed the progress of the news media as they wrangled for the best spots to set up their equipment.

Justin zoomed in for closer shots of the doctor.

The sixty-eight-year-old billionaire had earned degrees in medicine, political science, and business. An Angel Falls native, he spent most of his time traveling the world, investing in businesses and spending his fortune. He dressed with flair, sporting a panama hat, a cane, and a black cape draped over his huge shoulders.

Justin snapped another photo of Siffer, who was waving his black cane at one of the news technicians. The tip of the cane was a solid silver wolf's head, which Siffer was using as a cattle prod to get the crewman to move. One more thrust between the shoulder blades, and the man got the message and moved elsewhere.

Justin knew very little about the doctor beyond his generosity to GenEx Labs and his temper. Siffer's red hair and ruddy complexion became brighter as his level of excitement increased. This photo would have a bit more red in it, and Justin laughed at the thought of using a filter next time.

He snapped another shot of Siffer and several more of the river and surrounding area until he ran out of film.

"Made it," he said as he sat down on the walkway, removed the lens from the camera, and zipped it and the camera up inside the bag. He closed his eyes, and taking a deep breath, got back to his feet and steadied himself. The walk toward the stairs began well enough, but after a few steps, a wave of nausea hit him.

"Steady as she goes," he whispered after swallowing hard. Reaching the top stair, he opened his eyes, grabbed the railing, and forced himself to make his way down. It seemed to take an hour, but only a few minutes passed before his right foot softly touched the floor.

He sighed deeply, wiping beads of sweat, but Justin's hands still trembled slightly. A sense of relief overcame him when he saw his father approaching.

"Dad, you'll never believe..."

"I was watching and I'm proud of you. How many pictures did you get?"

"Almost a whole roll of the entire place. It was great."

"Make sure I get to see them when they're developed," his father said. He put his arm around Justin's shoulders and pulled him to one side. "Dr. Siffer's here; I'll introduce you."

They crossed the reception hall. From a distance, Justin noticed how odd Siffer looked in his sunglasses and driving gloves. He couldn't place the uneasy feeling his appearance gave.

"Lou," Mark began, "this is my son, Justin. You've heard me talk about him..."

"A pleasure to meet you, young man." The doctor's voice was deep and gravelly. Dr. Siffer extended a gloved hand and gave Justin the firmest handshake he had ever received. "Please pardon the glasses and gloves. Allergy medication for a skin problem makes my eyes sensitive. It will pass."

His unspoken questions answered, he asked, "Is it true you're going to announce today—"

"Yes, my candidacy for governor. You follow politics?" Siffer asked. He then quickly added, "Why of course, your camera! Your father told me about your fondness for photography and journalism."

"Yes, and-"

"I could use a local photographer," Siffer interrupted. "An apprentice—someone to capture various aspects of my campaign. I know someone at the Tribune who would be glad to work with you. You're out of school? I'll set up a meeting. For me, there is no such thing as too much positive press. Interested?"

"Yes and, uh, yes," Justin managed to get in.

"Justin just graduated. Tomorrow he turns eighteen," Mark explained. "We're having a combined birthday and graduation celebration this Saturday. We'd love to have you join us."

"This campaign eats up all my time," Siffer said. "In fact, time to go. I'll be back in three hours for the big event. Nice to meet you Justin - I'll set up that meeting."

With his cane held high and a brisk turn that caused his cape to rise and flow in his wake, Siffer made a hasty exit.

****

In another part of town, a mismatched duo appeared on Justin's front porch. Derrick Cartwright and Charles Phillip Underwood lived in the same neighborhood as Justin, just two streets over. Derrick had played football in his junior and senior years at Falls High. The former quarterback towered two feet above Charles. Nicknamed 'CPU', Charles was due to graduate in two years, being a grade ahead of other kids his age.

"Sorry boys," Jean Thyme, Justin's mom, explained. "Justin's with his dad."

"Will he be back soon?" Derrick asked.

"Not for a few hours - enough time for me to finish setting up for the party," Jean said, as she wiped her hands on an apron. "You boys coming?"

"Wouldn't miss it," CPU said, as he adjusted his wire-rimmed glasses. "Tell Justin we came by."

Derrick and CPU turned and walked back the way they had come.

"I'll bet Justin got to meet Dr. Siffer," CPU said as they turned down a side street.

"So?" Derrick shrugged, his new plan consisting of going home and raiding his refrigerator.

"He's one of the smartest people on Earth."

"I thought it was all those brains he has working for him. He's just the front man."

"You're crazy, Derrick," CPU said, shocked that someone he knew held such an opinion of the good doctor. "And he helps lots of people with all the money he gives away."

"Leverage," Derrick replied tersely. "And what's with those outfits?"

"He looks sophisticated."

"He doesn't do anything for me, so I don't really care much."

CPU, tired of being on the defensive with Derrick, again, changed the subject to something Derrick could immediately latch on to, "You have any pizza at your house?"

****

"Ten minutes to airtime," A voice shouted in the bustling halls of Gen Ex Labs. In that moment the lobby reminded Justin of a gigantic, buzzing beehive as technicians made last-minute preparations.

Justin gripped a yellow slip of paper, given to him by one of Sniffer's aides. Angel Falls Tribune appeared in bold letters on the top. Beneath it was the name of his contact, Beverly Heartstone, and a phone number. A hand-written note added, "Call her to set up a convenient time."

The buzzing began to lessen as most of the cameras and reporters were in place and ready. Two hundred specially screened citizens of Angel Falls had been invited to attend the proceedings, with a luncheon to follow. Everyone attending knew that Dr. Siffer planned to run for governor, but few suspected he would announce it during today's broadcast. With only minutes to go, no one could find the two key players, Doctors Thyme and Siffer.

****

Mark Thyme kept his cool.

"This is not the most opportune time to learn of this," Siffer, raspy and red-faced, barked at him. "With all these people here. And the press."

"Not one person, except my lab assistant, knows the vial is missing," Mark assured him.

"And the person who took it," Siffer said sarcastically. "Are the contents dangerous?"

"There's no danger to the general public, as long as the nanobots have not been programmed—and they haven't. The contents of the vial look like cooking oil. It's about as harmless."

"Keep me informed," Siffer fumed. "GenEx is supposed to have the tightest security in the world. A major security foul-up in a genetics lab would be a serious embarrassment for my campaign."

"It's probably a clerical error. It'll show up."

The missing vial was not much larger than a toilet paper tube. It might be easy to conceal, but security procedures ensured that it was impossible to get any test substances out of their assigned labs or anywhere near the front doors.

"My lab assistant is double-checking her lab entries now. I'll let you know what we find," Mark offered the enraged doctor. "In the meantime, they're waiting for us at the podium."

****

Despite the hours of preparation, the entire press conference lasted just fifteen minutes. Justin watched from the side of the room and noticed how small his father looked standing next to Siffer. Strangely, the man continued to wear his gloves and sunglasses for the cameras.

Siffer spoke eloquently about GenEx's life-saving work. The man's voice resonated, drawing them in as his cane rose and fell like a conductor's baton. He could easily mesmerize any audience. They were under his complete control.

As Justin watched the speech, a shiver suddenly ran up his spine. His head felt woozy, like it was buzzing. The feeling passed as quickly as it had come.

"No more climbing those stairs," he muttered out loud.

Without giving away any trade secrets, Siffer praised GenEx's latest project. He seemed to have a reasonable comprehension of the work, which enabled him to present most of the facts in a way that everyone could understand and appreciate. Justin thought that the doctor had to be the most knowledgeable man in the world. How else could he have earned all his degrees?

Siffer presented a brief history of GenEx Labs to a group of people who already knew it. It wasn't necessary for Siffer to blow his own horn, but it was an election year.

Fifteen years earlier, GenEx Labs had almost folded. Some blamed poor management, others, the political climate and a prevailing distrust of genetic research. The injection of Siffer's funds and reorganization had turned the place around within eight months.

Security became tighter under his guidance. New lab protocols were established and strictly enforced to protect the work and the employees. Public safety was paramount, but the less the public knew, the better.

Siffer boasted of the company's public relations department, which he had tripled in size to repair the company's bruised image. Justin, and everyone else listening, knew that GenEx Labs owed him an enormous debt. The company employed over sixty-five percent of the population of Angel Falls.

"And I want to see these advancements continue," Siffer concluded, "which is why I am presenting this check to GenEx Labs for the amount of twenty million dollars. Here's to your future success."

Accompanied by cheers and applause, Siffer looked directly into the cameras as he handed Mark

Thyme an oversized mock-up of the check. Mark smiled and held it up for everyone to see.

"On behalf of everyone at GenEx, we would like to thank you, Dr. Siffer, for your partnership in our efforts."

Mark left the podium with the cardboard check under his arm and disappeared into one of the elevators. Siffer remained, smiling and waving to his audience and the cameras.

"I have one more announcement," he said, waving his arms over his head to quiet the room. "You all know that I wear many hats, literally and figuratively."

Siffer paused a moment to allow for some polite laughter.

He continued, "Today I would like to add another hat, one which I will throw into the political ring, as I declare to you now, my intention to run for governor of this fine state!"

As the crowd cheered, Justin realized how lucky he was. With high school finally over, a major political candidate had just recommended him for a job in the field he loved. It felt as though the world was his.

Suddenly, he saw his father rush from one of the elevators, minus his white lab coat, clearly in a big hurry. Before slipping out of a rear exit, he motioned to Justin who understood to follow him.

Justin left from the front entrance and ran back to the lot where they had parked.

"What's up, dad?" he asked, as they both reached the car at the same time.

"Get   in.   We   have   a   problem."

Chapter 2

This was the place to be in times of trouble. It's funny, Justin thought, how things work. One second, the world is an all you can eat buffet. Then suddenly, you have food poisoning.

It was too early to know how the disappearance of the nanobots would affect his father's future. Mark Thyme, levelheaded under even the most difficult circumstances, had become quite anxious over this issue. His anxiety had now spread to his entire family. The loss had occurred under his watch: his lab and its security were ultimately his responsibility.

The vial was harmless in its present state, especially to the average person on the street. But nanobots could become extremely dangerous in hands that are more knowledgeable and less than scrupulous. That this breach had occurred in an age of terrorism made him all the more anxious.

Justin and Derrick stretched out against the old willow tree, shoes off, their toes touching the water. The lake extended out for miles in front of them, stirred by a warm breeze. Lazy ripples lapped at their feet. The grass rolled gently to and fro, while willow branches dangled and swayed, gently brushing the tops of their heads. Not a cloud could be seen in the sky.

From up here, the entire town spread out below them. A Great Blue heron glided down to land in the shallows of the lake before two others joined it. Justin had a renewed appreciation for this spot after yesterday's nightmare.

A comfortable drowsiness overcame him, brought on by the low roar of the waterfall behind the two boys, its mist gently spraying their faces every time the wind changed. Justin closed his eyes, drowsy from a night with too little sleep.

At three a.m. this morning he had turned eighteen, but he didn't yet feel any different. Tomorrow he'd celebrate his birthday and graduation with his friends. But here, in this spot, he could forget yesterday's more disturbing events at the lab. His family had faced some minor calamities in the past, but this one seemed to affect his father differently.

Justin started to doze off....

"They won't fire your dad, will they?" Derrick's words shattered the calm like a gunshot.

"Not now, Derrick," Justin grumbled.

"That new lab assistant - how much do they know about her? Have you ever met her?"

Justin normally appreciated Derrick's bulldog tenacity. It had gotten them out of a lot of scrapes in school.

But not today.

He wished he had the energy to throw the bulldog another bone in the hopes he'd drop this one.

"Haven't met her," Justin mumbled. He turned over to face away from Derrick and concentrate on the soothing rumble of the falls.

Derrick didn't take the hint, "Think about it. GenEx never had a security breach until someone from out of town got hired."

Justin tried to get comfortable, but his restful mood was rapidly fading.

The heron raised its head and suddenly lifted skyward, moving west towards another part of the lake. The two others followed.

"I'll bet Siffer's involved somehow; he'd like nothing better than to take complete control of GenEX. Isn't it the guilty ones who protest the loudest?"

Justin prepared himself to hear one of Derrick's conspiracy theories. He wondered how someone who was normally so levelheaded could come up with such off-the-wall ideas.

"Today GenEx, tomorrow the world," Justin said in mock apprehension.

"Make fun all you want, but there's something I don't like about that guy."

Justin sat up to face Derrick. "You'd better bring a life preserver, because you've just gone off into the deep end!"

"The real Siffer gets buried in the news. He can afford to buy off the media."

"I had forgotten that. According to you, being rich makes him the bad guy."

"'Money is the root of all evil…'"

"That's 'The love of money is the root of all evil'. Besides, Siffer gives most of his away."

Derrick backed down for the moment. He closed his eyes and folded his hands behind his head against the willow.

Justin appreciated the break. If events at the lab weren't stressing out his family, he might have enjoyed a bit of banter with Derrick over Doctor Siffer. He loved to goad Derrick about his politics, but not today.

The lake appeared bluer than usual. The sun sparkled in the ripples created by fish splashing the surface to catch water bugs. Bullfrogs barked back and forth. Out of the corner of his eye, Justin caught a glimpse of something in the distance.

Justin spent a lot of time up at the lake, but never gave any thought to the odd sculpture that he now observed. He had learned about it in history class and read more about it in some magazines from the fifty's in the library.

A large bronze angel stood behind a chair mounted on a concrete pedestal, wings spread wide.

The angel gripped the chair with both hands, maintaining its sentinel stare over Angel Falls to the east. In front of the angel, a golden sword pierced the chair from above, embedding itself in the concrete.

A tarnished bronze plaque on the pedestal held an inscription:

Having your conversation honest among

The Gentiles: that whereas they speak

Against you as evildoers, they may by

Your good works, which they shall be-

Hold, glorify God in the day of visitation.

The angel's head was barely visible above the wild berries and thicket that grew around the lake. For more than two hundred years, the monument allegedly bore witness to his hometown's beginnings.

According to legend, a visitation by angels and the hospitality of one man saved the town in its worst hour. For Justin, it had been nothing more than a dull eight-page report for one of his classes.

A search through the archives of the Angel Falls Tribune would often uncover a story about an attempt to steal the sword. Fewer such stories appeared in editions printed after 1975, when the

state placed the monument under the Park Service's jurisdiction and protection.

Many had tried, but the sword remained immovable, holding fast to the wood and stone for two centuries. Eventually people lost interest in the monument and the message of an angelic visitation had become a mere fairy tale told to children at bedtime.

Derrick must have been looking at the monument at the same time because he suddenly said, "Do you think angels actually visited this spot?"

"It's just a story," Justin said.

Derrick dug deeper. "So, evil—and now angels—they don't exist?"

"It's not something I think about much, Derrick."

"What about the devil?"

Justin turned suddenly and snapped, "Like some bogeyman creating trouble? We make our own trouble."

"But, spiritual warfare...."

"Is this about Siffer?"

"No. It's about you now. What do you believe?"

"Drop it. I came here for some quiet," Justin grunted and spun around to his side.

"Skeptic," Derrick yelled.

"Bulldog!" Justin shot back.

Justin forced his eyes shut with a "Humph", and Derrick slumped back against the tree.

Twenty minutes passed before Derrick reached behind his back and pulled an oddly shaped object from his knapsack, clumsily wrapped in gold foil paper.

"Here," Derrick mumbled. "Almost forgot." He tossed the package over to Justin.

Justin hesitated before unwrapping it. "It's not a bomb, is it?"

"Just open it."

Justin's mood changed from apprehension to curiosity as each piece of wrapping paper fell away. He smiled.

"A new camera bag."

"Yeah - that old duct-tapped thing doesn't go with your new job."

"This is great, but I haven't even been interviewed yet so it's not a sure thing. Besides, I've been getting negative vibes about this editor I'm supposed to see."

"With your buddy Siffer behind you, you can't lose."

"Hey, time out. He's not my buddy and I hear this Beverly Heartstone can be a real hard nose."

Justin examined the new camera bag. It had multiple pockets for storing spare lenses, the flash, film, and extra batteries. "It's real leather. This must have set you back a penny."

"I got a good deal at the grand opening of that new place downtown. You should check out the--"

Suddenly Justin sucked in a loud, raspy breath. The camera bag dropped from his hands and tumbled towards the lake.

"Justin, what's up?" Derrick gave Justin's shoulder a shove, but he was rigid, staring out across the lake, with a strange look on his face.

"You OK?" Derrick shook Justin harder this time, sending him tumbling over like a mannequin. "Justin!"

Chapter 3

Justin wearily submitted to his dad's examination in their living room. He was sure a truck had hit him. Now his father's medical bag sat next to him as Dr. Thyme probed, poked, and prodded. Derrick had managed to make it back without getting a speeding ticket but still looked shaken from the ordeal.

"It was like he wasn't breathing," Derrick told Justin's father.

"How long did it last?"

"I had to drag him to the car. He didn't snap out of it until we got here," Derrick said.

"It was worse than last night," Justin interrupted. He massaged both temples, making small circular motions with the heels of his hands.

His father frowned as he removed the blood pressure cuff. "Last night?" he asked. "What happened last night?"

"You've had enough to think about," Justin said.

"Your blood pressure's up, your pulse is irregular, and you've just lost several minutes of your life that you can't account for. Tell me what's going on."

"I couldn't sleep. The interview next week was on my mind," Justin began. "My head went woozy. Suddenly I'm remembering details from biology class, of all things. Only it was like I was actually there seeing everything that's happening!"

"Seeing things, like a photographic memory?" Derrick asked.

"I guess." Justin let his head drop into his hands and moaned. "It was really scary!"

His father finished checking him over and put his medical instruments away. "Your color is starting to return," he said. "I'd like to conduct a more thorough examination at the lab."

"All the stuff I couldn't remember for tests… now I remember," Justin said.

"The brain has a way of retaining everything," his father said. "But most of it gets buried; we can't always retrieve it when we want to."

"Not only that, my whole life was playing out in front of me. Even Animal Planet episodes. What's that about?"

"Too bad school's over," Derrick said and poked Justin's side. "You could've graduated summa cum something-or-other."

"Were you lightheaded or nauseous during this experience?" Mark Thyme frowned.

"There was just tingling between my ears, like something buzzing inside my head."

"Any heart palpitations, sweating, or flashes of light?"

"Nothing like that. And the thing that happened at the lake, it wasn't a memory. I don't know what that was."

"Can you describe it?"

Justin hesitated, "What if it happens again?"

"I'm right here if you need me," his father said. "I'll monitor your vital signs as you go."

With his father's finger on his pulse, Justin described how, like a silent video inside his head, a vision had played several times, fast-forwarding one moment and in slow motion the next. Figures appeared with distorted faces. Strange emotions held him captive, emotions that were not his own.

He could see a ghost, or something like a dark fog, swaying back and forth, flapping and hovering over a body stretched out flat, facing upwards. Another apparition floated in the same spot, watching. Chilling cold, like icy metal, gripped him during the vision.

The final, awful scene was a sharply focused face, bloodied and bruised, staring out at him with dead eyes.

Justin breathed a heavy sigh. Beads of perspiration appeared on his forehead and upper lip.

"It looked dead and it might have been a baby," he explained. "It was staring right at me."

His father's expression was not too comforting, nor was his request for Justin's arm. "I'm going to take some blood samples," he said.

Justin's arm trembled as he held it out.

Something occurred to him for the first time. He'd never known his biological parents and his medical history would be valuable right now. If any rare medical problems lurked in his family, he'd like to know about it.

"Do I have a brain tumor or something?" he asked.

After some difficulty getting the needle to puncture Justin's arm and locate a vein, his father said, "You certainly don't have a tumor, but let's get those tests done ASAP."

****

Mike Gordon wiped his sleeve across his sweaty forehead and loosened his tie. Two hours locked inside a small room with Lou Siffer was agitating enough, but now the air conditioning had shut down entirely.

The two men had been laboring over digitized security videos, which covered the most likely time the vial would have disappeared. The last in the set held their interest the longest. The other videos displayed a mostly empty lab, with little activity and nothing involving the vial directly. They were able to fast-forward through those. But this particular segment showed Mark's new assistant, Dawn Stoltzfus, running a series of tests on the nanobots.

They watched Dawn call up the vial on the computer. Moments later, a pneumatic tube built into the wall opened, revealing the vial. She reached for the container with her left hand and placed it in a rack as she typed instructions into the computer with her right hand.

When Dawn finished her scheduled tests, she called up the transport tube and placed the vial back into the tube with her left hand. Then, with her right hand, she accessed the computer to instruct the system to transport the vial safely back to the storage vault. After keying in the instructions, she turned to one side, allowing the camera to see her left hand again. She was writing standard procedural notes in her lab manual.

Except for the five minutes when Dawn actually handled the vial, its work cycle was fully automated and computerized. Transport, manipulation, and storage were controlled using robotics. More importantly, the vial was always in view during the entire process.

Gordon, obviously frustrated, spoke first. "It had to be somewhere in here, if it happened at all, Dr. Siffer. But you saw it yourself; nothing out of the ordinary happened."

"Yet a vial of our latest discovery is missing, just the same, isn't it?" Siffer said.

"Dawn did everything by the book," Gordon stressed. "You saw it yourself. Her written logs show it and yes, the vial is missing. I don't know how it possibly-"

"Video can be altered."

"Not possible. Our system of redundancy alone would prevent-"

"Never mind," Siffer interrupted. "You're head of security and I expect you to find that vial. Interview anyone who had anything remotely to do with Dr. Thyme's lab. Check the cleaning crew if necessary. If I complain to the board, you'll find yourself looking for work elsewhere."

"Threats won't solve anything," Gordon barely concealed the exasperation in his voice. "I'll check everything again, but I'm going to enlist the help of another set of eyes. A different perspective could help here. We'll check earlier time frames too, if we have to."

"I demand to be present during any further viewings," Siffer said.

"What's the point?"

"I will not suffer any embarrassment to my campaign and incompetent associations are an embarrassment, Mr. Gordon. This town is strategic to my plans and GenEx is its major focal point. I want to be involved. Understand? I need to know what others learn about the missing vial as they learn it."

"You want this to become your full-time job? That's what they pay me for. You don't need to be-"

"Just archive the video for now. Go back over the computer records and transcripts. If we need to look at this again, let me know. We'll schedule a viewing time when we can all be present."

"Sure. I'll keep you in the loop, if that's what you want. We'll get to the bottom of this, I can assure you!"

Gordon had enjoyed his current position for the last several years. What Siffer thought he could accomplish, aside from what his security personnel had already done, was beyond him. He owed his job to this infuriating man and the irony galled him.

He decided to make a copy of the video to view at home. It was against company policy, but he was desperate. He could lose his job if he was caught taking security information off the compound but, if Siffer got his way, he could lose it anyway. Gordon was resourceful and he could rig up something to get around the security's high-tech failsafe mechanisms.

He would also make sure he talked to Dawn Stoltzfus.

****

CPU turned ideas into slogans at his family's computer center. The phrase, "When you need a computer, go Hi Tech" was his idea and it played daily on the local radio stations. A bookstore and coffee house, which took up the far corner of the Hi Tech computer showroom, were also his ideas. Customers could buy, trade or read books and magazines at their leisure, while sipping their favorite blend of coffee. It was a popular place to hangout and Justin and Derrick spent most of their free time here when they weren't at the lake. Justin knew how to use a computer, but whenever it gave him trouble, he looked to Hi Tech to fix it. So when his laptop started locking up and generating strange error messages, he knew it was time to bring it to CPU. After two days without a computer, he was glad to get it back.

"It was a defective memory module," CPU explained. "I replaced the SODIMM and you're good to go."

"Whatever you just said, I don't care, as long as it works," Justin handed the computer to Derrick and reached for his wallet. CPU always got the job done right, even though Justin rarely understood his explanations.

"If you could keep Justin from locking up, you'd be a real superstar tech," Derrick said.

"I heard. Are you OK now?" CPU asked Justin.

"Who knows? My head still feels funny."

"He's a walking textbook - he'll be smart as you soon." Derrick grinned and quickly glanced at Justin.

"I'm not laughing," Justin shot back.

"You really remember everything word-for-word?" CPU asked.

"Seem to. Lot of good it does now."

"He still has the vision," Derrick said as he tried to untangle the power adapter and balance the laptop in his arms. "How long do you expect me to hold this thing for?"

"The vision doesn't come as often-"

"Hey, Justin," Derrick motioned with his head toward a stack of magazines. "Isn't that your dad's new assistant?"

Justin paid CPU and looked over.

"Her name's Dawn," CPU said. "From back east. Pennsylvania, I think. This is the third time she's been in here this week."

Justin could only see the back of her head. He knew she was about five foot two with thick auburn hair. "I thought dad's assistant would be older."

"She just moved here, right after attending a tech school," CPU said. "That would make her the youngest lab assistant GenEx has ever hired."

"Someone pulled some heavy-duty strings for her to get that job," Derrick said.

"You should talk to her," CPU suggested.

Derrick looked over at Dawn and back at Justin. "He's chicken."

Justin took a step in Dawn's direction and then stopped and pretended to count the change in his wallet.

"Chicken, like I said," Derrick repeated.

"Just ask her what it's like working for your dad. There's your excuse to go over," CPU said.

Justin's curiosity got to him and CPU's suggestion helped. He shoved his wallet into his back pocket and started over. Maybe she knew something about the missing nanobots that could help his father.

"I think I'll put this thing down," Derrick called to him. He rested the computer on the counter, as the boys watched Justin do something he'd never done before. Justin wasn't the type to initiate a conversation with a girl he didn't know.

Dawn, her face buried in a magazine, seemed completely unaware of his approach. He was just two feet away when he cleared his throat and said, "So what's it like working for my dad?"

Dawn looked up from her magazine to face him for the first time and smiled. As soon as their eyes met, something happened.

He never heard her say, "You must be Justin!"

Chapter 4

Reality slowly crept back into Justin's brain as he awoke in a small room across from two empty beds similar to the one he was lying on.

He was alone.

An airtight door separated his room from a much larger area, visible through a pair of thick bay windows. Besides the sinks, microscopes, and cabinets above him, other equipment he didn't recognize filled the room. Nobody was there; the lights in the other room were off.

Icy fingers danced up and down his back. He shook the cold feeling with a shudder.

The constant hiss of air from the exchange system meant the place hadn't been abandoned. Then he realized he was in the GenEx infirmary, a fact that offered little comfort.

His stomach cramped with a nauseating dread. His arms and legs flushed with a tingling sensation, as if they were falling asleep.

What's happening?

With a sudden hiss, his father burst through the airtight doors and stood by Justin's bed. He looked down at his son, who was barely able to sit up, and spoke. "You're conscious. How're you feeling?"

"Not so good."

"This is the best-equipped place to find out what's been happening to you." His father sat on the bed next to him. "You blacked out. Can you remember anything?"

"I made a complete idiot of myself."

"You gave everyone quite a scare. Dawn was asking about you."

"I just went over to say hello."

"She said you looked pale and suddenly fell over."

"I was fine until she looked at me. I mean, as soon as I looked into her eyes, my head filled up with all kinds of feelings."

"Like what?"

"Not sure; they weren't mine. They were Dawn's. It felt like she's sad - afraid."

"You're saying Dawn was feeling these things, not you?"

"It was as if for a moment I could see into her head. It only lasted a second. I don't remember anything after that."

"At least you suffered no injuries when you fell. Good thing Derrick's quick on his feet - he was the one that caught you."

"He's recovered a lot of fumbles. I sure freaked out Dawn."

"She'll just be glad to hear you're OK. She was concerned." His father smiled and nudged him with his elbow, "Just don't pass out on her next time!"

Justin fell back onto the infirmary bed, exhausted. The sense of Dawn still lingered, fresh in his mind. Somehow he knew her, even though they had never met until that moment. He wasn't sure there would be a 'next time'.

His mind drifted until a GenEx technician entered the infirmary frantically waving a brown folder. He recognized Jim Wilson, a friend of his dad's. He had an odd expression on his face that sent another wave of nausea washing over Justin. He swallowed hard.

Wilson called over, "You're going to want to see this, Mark. It has some, uh, you really need to look at this!"

His father took the folder while Jim fidgeted with his pen and looked at the ceiling. The answers Doctor Thyme hoped to find in this report only created more questions.

"Justin, would you excuse us for a minute?"

"What's up, dad?"

"Nothing, just a mini conference. I'll be right outside these doors if you need anything."

The doors swooshed and hissed shut as his father left the infirmary. He felt the room's air pressure change inside his ears. It was quiet and lonely again. When the buzzing in his head returned, he closed his eyes and rested on the bed, hoping that his father would be back shortly with good news.

To pass the time he thought about Dawn. The mental images he had encountered when he approached her were beginning to fade, but he could still see her eyes. Her eyes, the most beautiful he'd ever seen, had a devastating effect on him.

Justin tried to imagine the voice that went with those eyes. It had to be sweet, soothing. He closed his eyes and pictured her moving gracefully about the room and it put him at ease.

How long he lay there resting, he didn't know. When he looked out toward the lab, his father and the technician were still having a rather animated discussion. He tried to hear what they were saying, but his room was not only airtight, but completely soundproof.

****

Jim Wilson was obviously having a difficult time hiding his excitement. Mark flipped through the files he had been handed, but did not look quite as excited by what he was reading.

"It's amazing," Jim said.

"I know. You said that already," Mark waited for Jim to get to the point.

"Just amazing. His bone density is off the charts."

"Are you sure?"

"I'm telling you, the subject's bones are like light-weight steel rods."

"Justin. His name is Justin - my boy, remember?"

"Sorry, Dr. Thyme."

Mark was afraid to ask, but the look on Jim's face told him there was more. "Forget it. What else have you got?"

"Look at this," Jim held up an x-ray. "The bone formations. Unusual—see here? And look here?"

Mark examined the x-ray, particularly the area around Justin's shoulder blades.

"Don't you see it?" Jim asked. "Here, these processes in the bones. Look at the shape and size of the shoulder blades themselves. These are characteristic of birds."

"Justin doesn't have wings and he's not a bird. If it's a birth defect, it's a minor one that hasn't affected Justin's ability to function normally."

"Of course. But we don't know the boy's father. Could he have been an ostrich?"

"Not funny, Jim."

"Sorry again, Dr. Thyme. There are just too many genetic oddities to ignore."

"Look," Mark asked, "can you assure me the nanobots had nothing to do with these 'oddities', as you call them. Or the blackouts?"

"Sudden memory increase may be the result of a nanobot function. Increased stamina too. But there is more going on here than nanobots alone can explain," Jim said. "What you hold in your hands looks more like the profile of a genetically altered human being."

"Altered. How? You sound like there might be something strange in our drinking water? If nanobots are not responsible for this, what is?"

"You said he was adopted. Is there any family history that could shed some light on this?"

Mark shook his head. It suddenly struck him that he had never known the finer details of Justin's family. When Justin's biological mother had died, she had been cremated, which meant that exhuming her body for further study would be impossible.

"Another thing. We broke three needles before we were finally able to get a blood sample. Justin's skin has become virtually puncture-proof."

Mark handed the reports back to Jim. "I saw the micro-scan. The dermis had a chain-link structure."

"Like the chain mail medieval knights wore for protection. Very pliable, but not penetrable."

"Cancerous?"

"Absolutely not. In fact, Justin's health is perfect."

"If I didn't know better, I'd say the reported DNA anomalies were fabricated, but now...."

Jim tucked the reports under his arm. "Your son does present us with a bit of a mystery, sir."

****

Justin sat up when the airtight doors swooshed again and his father returned to the infirmary. "Can we get out of here now?"

"There's something I need to do and then we'll be out of here. Sorry, it will just be a few more minutes."

"Dad, did Dawn's father die when she was younger?"

"Well yes, but it's not common knowledge. How did you know?"

"I   saw   it   in   her   eyes."

Chapter 5

The police found the body of Mike Gordon, forty-eight, on the sidewalk outside his apartment complex, late on Saturday evening.

"Who's in charge here?" asked the officer who had first discovered Mike's body.

Among the suits milling around, taking samples and pictures below the apartment, one looked up. Detective Tom Selden walked over to the officer.

"You have something for me?" Tom asked.

"Someone tampered with the bolts on the balcony railing," said the officer, as he flipped through some notes taken earlier at the scene. "See these teeth marks?" He produced a black, wrought iron bolt, partially sawn through and showed it to Tom. "That thing broke away real easy."

"Any signs of a break-in?" Tom asked.

"He probably knew his assailant. There were no signs of a struggle and the door was not jimmied." The officer flipped his notebook closed and stuffed it into his front pocket. "That's all I got. Coroner's got him now, the rest is yours."

Tom looked around at the scene, checked his watch, and half-facetiously said, "Thanks." An already spoiled evening was about to drag on and he was tired. No immediate suspects and GenEx politics would be difficult to plow through. This was going to be a drawn-out, thorny case.

****

The news of Gordon's murder in the Sunday edition of the Angel Falls Tribune made state and national headlines. It also let the missing nanobot 'cat' out of the bag.

Siffer's inflammatory statements in the press stirred up a bee's nest at GenEx. He slowly started to distance himself from the company. Implicitly accusing Gordon of terrorist activities, he stated that, "Recent dealings with Gordon created grave doubts in my mind about his loyalties and his suitability for his position."

After church, Justin avoided Derrick and left by a side door. He was afraid he might hear another one of Derrick's lectures and wasn't in the mood. Everyone else left through the front door to shake Pastor Greenfield's hand.

As he stood behind some tall bushes, Justin could just about hear what people were saying. He recognized the voice of Joshua Hardy, Angel Falls' oldest citizen. Mr. Hardy was reliving the old days with the Pastor.

Mr. Hardy said, "This building has stood here for a hundred and twenty-five years. My daddy helped build it."

"Yes, I was aware of that, Mr. Hardy," Pastor Greenfield said. "It's one of the oldest buildings in Angel Falls and it's still standing, albeit with a few renovations."

Justin didn't usually pay much attention to Mr. Hardy, but he had nothing better to do while waiting for everyone to leave. They seemed especially slow to leave today and so far, there was no sign of Derrick.

Hardy's granddaughter, Melissa Allen, interrupted the conversation her grandfather and the pastor were having. "Granddad, other people are waiting to greet the pastor. We'd better get home for dinner. Good sermon, Pastor Greenfield."

"I liked it too." It was Derrick.

Justin peeked around to the front corner of the building in time to see Derrick heading his way, so he raced around to the back, near the parking lot. After some time weaving in and out among some vans, a searing pain suddenly shot across his foot.

Hardy's wheelchair had rolled over Justin's foot and sent Justin tumbling on top of the old man. Hardy couldn't have weighed more than one hundred and thirty pounds, wheelchair and all.

Justin quickly jumped up from the chair and stepped back to make sure that Mr. Hardy was still alive.

"No, my foot's fine, really!" Justin told Melissa. "It was my fault. I should watch where I'm going."

Suddenly Derrick showed up. "Hey buddy, where've you been?"

"Right here, falling on top of Mr. Hardy," Justin said sheepishly.

"It's OK, Justin, we're fine," Melissa said. "You remember my granddad, don't you?"

Justin grinned awkwardly. "After today, he'll be hard to forget."

Justin held out his hand and Mr. Hardy looked up to reach for it. They made contact and suddenly Mr. Hardy's eyes widened; he gasped and started to wheeze. Justin thought the man was having a heart attack.

"The Heritage." Hardy wheezed.

Justin quickly released Hardy's hand. He looked imploringly at Melissa for help.

"Nephilim," Hardy wheezed, before fainting, apparently from exhaustion.

"It's OK, Justin. I think granddad just needs to get back home and rest. He's had a busy day."

Melissa wheeled her grandfather toward her specially equipped van. Mr. Hardy, apparently revived from his faint, looked very animated, waving his arms and rambling excitedly.

Justin just stood and watched him leave, dumbfounded.

"You look like someone just pushed you out of a plane without a parachute," Derrick remarked.

Justin tried to regain his composure. "Old people can be scary."

"You sure made quite an impression on the old guy –literally," Derrick laughed.

"Yeah, right. I though he was having a stroke or something. What was he saying, anyway?"

"'Nephilim'. It's in Genesis."

"Genesis?"

"You know, the Bible? Duh."

"Knock it off! I know what Genesis is; I just don't remember seeing anything about Nepha-whatsis."

"Ne-pha-leem," Derrick enunciated slowly.

"Who cares?" Justin said, pronouncing the conversation closed. He shoved his hands down his pants pockets and started for home on foot.

After several minutes of watching the sidewalk pass under his feet, Justin heard Derrick say, "It was a great party yesterday."

"You're still here?"

"Sure, I'm eating dinner at your house today. Remember?"

Justin shrugged. "Right."

"Your mom's a good cook. Birthday and graduation presents in one day - must be nice."

After a few more minutes of silence, Derrick asked, "What was it your dad wanted to talk to you about, after church?"

"Maybe he's found out what's wrong with me."

"On the plus side, it can't be too horrible, or he would have told you sooner," Derrick said.

Derrick's attempts at optimism were of little comfort.

"Maybe he's quitting GenEx," Derrick said.

"No way!"

"They were friends, your dad and Mike Gordon?" Derrick asked.

"Yeah, sort of."

"I'll bet Siffer is blowing a gasket over this."

"Dad can't wait to get back to work tomorrow," Justin said facetiously.

Justin's mom and dad had attended an earlier church service and were at home preparing Sunday dinner. When the boys arrived, everything was ready and Derrick stayed, as he often did on Sunday afternoons. When they had finished eating, Justin felt a sudden urge to know more about his past.

Justin remembered that his mother and father kept their wedding album in an old cedar chest by the fireplace. The contents of the cedar chest had never interested him—until now.

He opened up the large chest and dug deep down inside. He went past layers of blankets, old newspapers, books and a few family heirlooms until he found the wedding album. When he picked it up and opened it, a manila envelope fell out.

Derrick picked it up and found some black and white photos and newspaper clippings inside. "These are pretty old looking. Who's this?" He handed one of the pictures to Justin.

"Mom, who's in these pictures?"

Jean came over and examined the photos for a moment until recognition suddenly set in. "Oh dear. I forgot we had these."

She called to Mark, who immediately knew what had happened by the look on his wife's face and the open cedar chest.

"It's funny you would find these now, Justin," his father said. "What timing."

"Is mom upset? Who is this woman in the pictures?"

"Should I come back some other time, Dr. Thyme?" Derrick asked, sensing that this might turn into a serious family discussion.

"I'll leave that up to Justin - it has to do with what I wanted to talk to you about."

"Stay, Derrick. I think it's about my birth mother."

His father handed the pictures back and said, "That's part of it."

Mark motioned everyone to take a seat and proceeded to explain about the woman in the photographs. She was Justin's biological mother, although she did not exactly give birth to him.

She had aborted him.

Justin was floored, hearing this for the first time. "How could she?" He asked.

"She was hysterical when we first met her, just hours after the abortion. She acted like someone wanted either her child, or her, dead."

"Or both," Jean added.

Justin, speechless, continued to stare at the photos in his father's hand.

"Your mother was almost six months pregnant, so they performed a C-section abortion. Later, the assisting nurse had a change of heart and went back to see if you were still alive. You weighed only two and a half pounds."

The face of the woman who would have been his mother burned into his mind. "She wanted to kill me...."

"I don't think so. Someone may have pressured her into it. Being terrified and alone, she didn't know who to trust."

"Who was she afraid of?" Justin asked.

"We never found out. She disappeared three weeks later. Afterwards, we learned she committed suicide. She was extremely unstable—"

Justin's dad stopped in mid-sentence and looked out of the window.

"What is it, dad?"

"Nothing."

"It looked like something," Justin said.

His father hesitated and finally said, "It occurred to me...the circumstances surrounding her death...there are similarities between her death and Gordon's."

"She might not have committed suicide?" Derrick asked.

"She insisted she had been threatened," Justin's mom said. "We thought it was drug-induced paranoia. She was such an irrational young woman."

"She was found in the street below the fourth-floor balcony of her hotel room," Justin's dad said.

"Was she pushed? Could there be a connection between the two — Gordon and Justin's mom, I mean?" Derrick asked.

"I don't know, Derrick. That's a bit of a stretch. But it is odd that these two deaths, eighteen years apart, have you in common, Justin. Neither crime has been solved."

"What's Justin got to do with Gordon?" Derrick asked.

"It's the GenEx connection, I'm afraid," Dr. Thyme said.

Derrick perked up. "Your vision at the lake. Justin, it's you."

"Which is where the connection comes in and it's the other thing I wanted to explain to you," Mark said. "Your vision may be a flashback of the abortion experience."

51

"How?" Justin asked.

"I took steps immediately after the abortion to help you recover. I believe those steps - an experimental medical procedure at the time - enabled you to experience the flashbacks during these last few days. The results of your recent blood tests indicate..."

"What experiment? How could something done that long ago suddenly cause me problems now?" Justin asked.

"The experimental treatment was meant to give you a fighting chance at a recovery, but it appears to have remained in your blood all these years and become active again. It's probably responsible for your enhanced memory."

Dr. Thyme explained how the abortionist's nurse, who snatched Justin from the abortion clinic, heard about Doctor Thyme's experimental research at GenEx Labs.

"You were near death and bleeding pretty heavily. The scar on your chin was the result of carelessness on the abortionist's part. Your mother was not in very good shape either, after he had finished with her," his father said.

"The nurse wrapped you up in a blanket and got you to me quickly. At GenEx, I injected you with a serum of nanobots."

Justin's face turned into a pale collage of disgust and horror. "The things stolen from the lab?"

"Very similar. Their purpose was to sustain you until your body could sustain itself and then dissipate from your system. Instead, they've multiplied and reactivated. Don't ask me how or why. They not only did their job keeping you alive, they appear to be more active now than ever. They've enhanced your mental and physical capabilities."

"Is that why his memory is so clear?" Derrick asked.

"Yes. It could also explain the buzzing in your head. That should disappear once you've become accustomed to their presence."

"At least it isn't a brain tumor," Derrick said.

Justin rubbed the back of his neck. "Right. Not much of a comfort, though. Who wants millions of little bugs squirming around inside them?"

"None of this explains Justin's claim to read Dawn's mind, or the visions, does it?" Jean asked her husband.

"I initially feared that Justin might be having a negative reaction to the nanobots, causing confusion or even psychosis."

Justin's jaw dropped.

"Now wait, Justin. I've since realized this is not the case, so take it easy." His father continued, "The nanobots are not responsible for your visions or other 'perceptions'. All they can do is give you increased memory, stamina, and endurance. I ran additional tests at the lab - DNA tests, a whole bio-scan..."

Justin braced himself.

"The results were not entirely normal."

Chapter 6

"Siffer's Campaign Headquarters", the receptionist answered tersely. She put the call on hold and muttered something under her breath. Unlike the other banks of phones, manned by volunteers, this was Siffer's personal line. Politicians, the press, and Political Action Committees, everyone sought a hearing with the Doctor. Ruth Hemsley's training guaranteed that only the most important calls would get through.

She normally forwarded other calls to volunteers, authorized to deal with lesser matters. After forcing the caller on the other end to wait a bit longer, Ruth picked up the line again.

"I'm sorry, Dr. Siffer is not available right...." Suddenly Ruth recognized the voice on the other end. "My apologies. Let me put you through - hold on one second."

Siffer glared at the four television sets on his office wall, each set to the latest election news. One of several newspapers on his desk reported an unprecedented thirty-five percent increase since yesterday in his statewide popularity.

There were still a few major holdouts, but he knew that Angel Falls would learn to love him. His hometown held the key that would convince the rest of the state to vote for him. He smiled. Most of his time was spent analyzing the positions of other powerful key players across the state. His powers of persuasion would sway them in his direction and the governorship would be his, whatever the cost.

The election had to be his, Siffer reasoned, as he rubbed his thumb back across the silver fox on the end of his cane. His work wouldn't end once he sat in the governor's chair. And decades of calculating would take him even further.

Much further.

"Dr. Siffer, that woman wishes to speak to you again," Ruth's voice broke in over the phone speaker.

Lou tossed the newspaper to his desk, punched the line, and picked up the receiver, "It's me. What have you got?"

He listened in one ear to the voice on the other end, while catching snatches of television news in the other.

"He's stronger than we thought," Siffer said to the caller. "Can you handle him?"

A special announcement suddenly appeared on one of the channels. Siffer interrupted, "Hold on, I want to hear this."

Siffer's ruddy face broke into a distorted smile.

One of the state's senators, vehemently opposed to Siffer's position on most issues, now threw in his support for the candidate from Angel Falls. Reporters were having a field day with this unexpected turn of events.

Returning his attention to the woman on the phone, Siffer said, "Williams is ours, you hear me? Yeah, we got him! But this other problem, get in closer. Timing is everything. I must maintain a hands-off approach for now." His smile faded into a scowl, his grip tightened on the receiver.

"This loose end has been a thorn in my side for far too long." The man thought to himself.

"You're very charming, so use your powers of persuasion. Understand?"

Siffer slammed the receiver down as an update on Gordon's death appeared on one of the TV screens. Even after two weeks, the police had no suspects in the case. They still considered it a murder investigation, but the evidence meant they were not ready to rule out suicide completely.

Grasping at straws, some reports were speculating that Gordon had tampered with his own railing to facilitate throwing himself off the balcony. He was, after all, too heavy to haul himself over the top, so he loosened it to crash through it.

"Foolish nonsense," Siffer huffed. He yanked the handkerchief from his vest pocket and wiped the sweat from his brow. The handkerchief had been getting a lot of use lately. He regained control and remained resolute. Everything was in motion and his plan couldn't fail.

Yet, that one loose end nagged at him.

Pounding his fist on his desk, Siffer grabbed the paper back up and resumed scanning the Tribune. "This police force needs a kick in the pants."

****

Justin and Derrick met up with CPU at Hi Tech. Sitting in a booth, sipping sodas, CPU got the latest on Justin, nanobots and all. Justin's untouched, thirty-two ounce soda, sat in front of him, flat and fizz-free.

"You're healthy as a moose. You'll probably live to be a thousand," Derrick said.

CPU kept giving Justin sideways glances

"Quit staring Charles, you're creeping me out."

"Don't get him mad, he might turn green and start breaking things," Derrick said.

CPU laughed, but quickly said, "It's probably nothing, Justin, don't sweat it!"

Justin looked at him. "Which do you mean, the 'abnormal' part or the 'nanobot' part?"

"'Nephilim'. That's what Mr. Hardy called you," Derrick said.

"Or the 'angel from outer space' part?" Justin grunted.

CPU sat straight up, eyes wide. He turned toward Derrick. "What about Nephilim?"

"Hardy said Justin was one," Derrick explained very casually.

Justin interrupted, "He'd been in the sun too long that morning!"

CPU started to wriggle agitatedly in the booth, kicking Derrick and almost spilling his soda.

"Hey, watch it. What's your problem?" Derrick cast a puzzled looked over at Justin. "What's he mumbling about?"

Justin grabbed CPU's shoulder to stop him from causing further spills. "You want to slow down and tell us what's got you all hyped up?"

"Why couldn't it happen here?" CPU asked.

"Why couldn't what happen?" Justin asked.

"It's all there."

"What's there? What is?" Derrick asked. CPU started to wriggle again.

Derrick's arm came down on CPU's head. "Cut it out."

CPU fell back into his seat, calmed down for the moment, and explained. "This town's history, the Bible, everthing. It's the legend. It's Justin!

"What does the history of Angel Falls have to do with the Bible or Justin?" Derrick asked.

"We need to visit Mr. Hardy to get the full story," CPU said.

"What story?" Derrick demanded.

"Does this have something to do with me?" Justin asked.

CPU's face was full of anticipation. "With you, us - possibly the whole world."

Chapter 7

Justin, Derrick, and CPU, like modern-day Three Musketeers, stood outside Melissa Allen's home. Several days a week Melissa went to the retirement center to bring her grandfather home for a visit.

When the door opened, CPU said, "Hi Mrs. Allen, is Mr. Hardy visiting with you today?"

"He sure is boys, come on in. Did you want to talk to granddad?" She held the door wide as the three marched inside.

"We could come back some other time if today's no good?" Justin said.

"Nonsense. Granddad would love visitors. He's resting in the living room. Come on in."

"Just don't sit on him or nothing, Justin," Derrick quipped.

"This is a surprise!" Melissa said. "Charles, I haven't seen you since you were a preschooler in diapers."

CPU blushed. "I help run the computer store now."

"I hear the ads on the radio every day; you must be doing great business. And Derrick, what have you been up to?"

"Helping dad at the auto repair shop. I start classes in business at Angel Falls University this fall."

"And Justin, I can't believe how tall you've gotten. Do you boys want some pecan pie?"

Derrick and CPU took some pie, but Justin politely declined. His stomach was starting to tie up in knots and he wasn't exactly in the mood to socialize. He just wanted some answers and he hoped that Melissa would have them. If he absolutely had to, he would approach Mr. Hardy, but after last Sunday, he was afraid to go near him.

"Something's on your mind, Justin. Anyone who turns down a piece of pie must have something on his mind," Melissa said, as she passed out plates and forks.

Justin took a seat and eyed the pie. "What was Mr. Hardy talking about last Sunday?"

Derrick and CPU accepted a glass of iced tea to go along with the pie. Justin, feeling dry-mouthed, took one too.

"I wasn't really paying attention, Justin. Sometimes he forgets where he is and starts reliving old memories. Your little run-in must have triggered one of them."

"He seemed pretty upset," Justin said.

62

"Having someone fall on you would do that," Derrick said with a mouthful of pie.

Justin ignored the comment. "What's 'Nephilim'?" he asked.

Melissa sighed. "I thought granddad was over that silly notion since he hasn't mentioned it for more than thirty years!" She offered them a second piece of pie and a refill of iced tea. The boys graciously declined both.

"That's Old Testament stuff," CPU said. "They're the offspring of angels and humans."

Melissa said, "Granddad's hobby is studying history. Living in this town all his life got him interested in the legend associated with it. Nobody I know remembers the stories associated with Angel Falls. Granddad didn't either, except after years of digging into old records. His research finally convinced him that the legend was true."

"That angels actually came here hundreds of years ago to save the town?" CPU asked.

"I'm surprised someone your age knows anything about it," Melissa said.

"I'm sort of a history buff myself," CPU said.

Justin became impatient and broke into their conversation. "What does all this have to do with me?" He asked.

"You'll have to ask granddad for the details, Justin," Melissa said. "Now that I think about it, granddad's mentioned you a couple of times since

Sunday. He'd probably enjoy a chance to explain all of this."

That was exactly what Justin was afraid of.

Melissa led the boys into the living room where Mr. Hardy was comfortably situated on the living room couch, his wheelchair folded in a corner. A Classics Greatest Hits album played softly in the background.

"Granddad, look who's here." Melissa guided the boys to chairs while Mr. Hardy took a moment to recognize his visitors. "This is Charles Underwood, Derrick Cartwright, and you remember Justin..."

Hardy nodded as Melissa introduced the boys, but when he saw Justin, he tried to stand up.

Melissa gently guided him back down to a sitting position, "No granddad, take it easy. Justin, why don't you sit on the couch next to my grandfather?"

Justin reluctantly took a seat on the couch and Mr. Hardy reached for his hand. For a guy his age, his handshake was surprisingly vigorous.

The old man came instantly to life as his eyes changed from sleepy to intense. "Justin Thyme. Mark and Jean's boy, how old are you by now?"

"Just turned eighteen las week, Mr. Hardy."

"Right, eighteen. Your mother would be..." Hardy searched the ceiling as he added up the years, "Thirty-seven!"

"Actually, she's forty-eight," Justin said.

"No, your biological mother. She was nineteen when she had you."

"You knew her?" Justin leaned in just a bit closer to the old man. "Other than mom and dad, you're the only other person I know who did."

"Your dad and I counseled her before she disappeared. She was in such a state. Afraid of her own shadow."

"What's the 'Nephilim'?"

Hardy examined Justin. "Evidence suggests that you are."

Justin was afraid he might be losing Mr. Hardy to dementia, but he continued to listen, despite his doubts.

Hardy explained how he had been able to get enough information from Justin's mother to conduct a genealogical search of her family. Her name was Sarah Kelly. Sarah was a direct descendant of Rachel Alda, daughter of an early settler of Grangeville.

CPU added some information of his own. "Angel Falls used to be called Grangeville, back in the late 1700s."

Hardy looked at CPU with interest. "Another young historian?" He asked.

"He just knows everything," Derrick said. "Especially computers."

"I know Visitation Lake appeared after the angels left," CPU added. "The water fall and river it created saved the town from drought and starvation."

"That's the gist of it," Hardy said. "The town changed its name and the new waterfall was named in honor of the angels."

"I thought those kind of things stopped happening two thousand years ago," Justin said.

"Geological surveys and other information I've dug up over the decades sure point to some miraculous event that changed the history of a dying settlement," Hardy said.

"What's the connection to me?" Justin asked.

Mr. Hardy winked at CPU and Derrick then turned to face Justin. "One of those angelic visitors had a child with Rachel Alda."

Justin's face twisted into one that said, "That's crazy."

"So that's how Justin got the Nephilim gene," Derrick said.

"Why me and why now?" Justin demanded. "You're talking about events that, if they really happened, happened a real long time ago!"

For another hour, the boys listened, spellbound, as Hardy wove fact and speculation into the history of Angel Falls and its connection to Justin.

"The evidence might be sparse, but I'm convinced that Angel Falls has had its share of extraordinary citizens over the last three hundred years.

"For starters, some old town records suggest that Rachel's boy was quite charismatic and could do some extraordinary things. Subsequently, the history of the town was dotted with the random appearances of exceptional individuals who possessed unusual abilities. You can check it out for yourself: the library has dozens of old records and newspapers on microfiche.

"The Nephilim gene seemed to skip generations, appear and then disappear, as if it had a will of its own. It has been a long time since one of these gifted individuals has made an appearance. All I can say is, it's about time you arrived, Justin. When you fell on me the other day I experienced an overwhelming sense in my spirit that you were the expected one."

"Why would an angel marry a human? It's hard enough to believe that angels came here in the first place," Justin said.

"Grangeville almost died. That's history," Hardy said. "The Aldas recorded a visit by two men. They knew they had only a short time left to live, the drought was so severe."

Hardy coughed, took a deep breath and continued, a little slower now.

"The angelic visitors left with a promise of hope for the town. The next day, the Aldas found an enormous lake in their front yard; an endless source of water fed by a newly created underground spring."

Hardy finished and sank back into the couch, but looked as eager as ever to talk.

CPU was able to fill in additional details. He explained how scientists had tried to pin the lake's appearance on a geological fault line below the plateau. When it shifted, a portion of an underground spring changed course and found its way to the surface. Erosion created the lakebed and the ongoing supply of water created the waterfall and river that continued to flow east through town. They later became known as Angel Falls and Falls River.

"But we know better," CPU concluded.

Switching gears, Justin asked, "Who was my mother so afraid of?"

"You heard about that?" Hardy's tone was sympathetic. He slowly raised a hand to rest on Justin's shoulder. "She wasn't around long enough for us to find out, but I'm inclined to put the blame on the abortionist."

"Do you think he murdered her too?"

"Personally, yes. But there was no evidence. With your mother gone, that mystery died with her."

Hardy lowered his hand and closed his eyes. For several minutes, he sat resting while the boys talked quietly among themselves. He perked up again when Derrick asked, "What's with the statue up by the lake?"

"Good question, young man." Hardy leaned forward slowly, eyes wide, mind alert again. "Alastair Alda was the best carpenter of his day. He made fine furniture. That chair in the statue is one of his originals. It's real weather-beaten, but it's survived more than three hundred years. Anyway, shortly after Rachel Alda died, the angel left, but first he pierced the chair with the sword."

"I've touched an angel's sword," CPU blurted excitedly.

"It's a weird-looking conglomeration of junk. What'd he do that for?" Derrick asked.

"I suppose as a warning," Hardy answered, "against evil forces ever trying to take control of Angel Falls."

Justin noticed that the old man was getting tired, but Hardy continued, "It's said that only a Nephilim can remove the sword."

"Where does Justin fit in?" CPU asked.

Hardy sighed and sank back into the couch. He looked more than just tired from excitement. Justin sensed some dark thing had suddenly sapped the man's energy.

The oldest man in town gasped, "Justin must save Angel Falls from its darkest hour." and passed out.

Chapter 8

Justin could have flipped through Hi Tech's magazines upside-down and they would have made as much sense as they currently did right side up. He skimmed through them anyway while CPU, enjoying some time-off from work, opened his laptop and logged onto the Internet. The Hi Tech lounge offered customers a wireless connection for a dollar an hour but the router was down. Until he could fix it, CPU got around the problem by connecting his cell phone to the laptop. It was like dialing out through an external modem.

"I wanted to learn more about nanobots, Angel Falls, and your mom. With Google's help I searched all night," CPU said.

Derrick slapped CPU on the back, causing his glasses to slide down his nose. "The little geek's good. What'd ya find?"

Tapping keys with one hand and fixing his glasses with the other, CPU explained, "With the proper transmitter frequency and code, the nanobots can be programmed to do all kinds of things, wirelessly."

"Big Yipp. Maybe we can get them to make me a cold Frappuccino," Justin balked.

CPU forced a grin. "Sorry, the machine's busted. Should be back up by tomorrow."

"Ignore him," Derrick told CPU. "What else did Gargoyle come up with?"

CPU's fingers never stopped flying across the keyboard and, without looking up, said rather severely, "It's Google, Derrick, not Gargoyle."

"Take it easy, I'm just playing with you, Braniac."

CPU continued with his findings, "Nanobots do more than carry oxygen. They can be programmed to zap the nerves with jolts of electricity."

"What for?" Derrick asked.

"It's experimental but they could fix damaged nerves and stuff."

"How are those things put inside someone?" Justin asked.

"Normally by injection directly into the affected nerve cluster or organ, depending on what job they're meant to do. Sometimes they're ingested."

Derrick twisted his face into a look of disgust. "As in, eaten?"

"Yup. Swallowed." CPU said.

Derrick looked like he was going to throw up. "Who'd drink that stuff?"

"They're tiny and tasteless. But as long as they get into the blood, they'll do whatever they're programmed for and go wherever they're needed." CPU said.

Justin changed the subject. "What about my mother?"

"Sarah Kelly? I found a direct link from Rachel Alda to her. Some of the genealogies list Rachel's husband as 'unknown'. Others list someone named Micah, which was a common name back then. No last name."

"Is he the angel?" Justin asked.

"Let's just say I looked everywhere and found out nothing about him. The information is incomplete. It's as if he never really existed."

"Then old Mr. Hardy was right," Justin said.

"I got the name of the nurse who brought you to GenEx...."

Justin's mood suddenly livened. "Really? No kidding?"

"And she's still alive in a nursing home only twenty miles from here in Ashland."

"I feel a day-trip coming," Derrick said.

Justin rubbed the scar under his chin. He wasn't being completely honest with everyone, but how much should he tell his friends about his own dealings with the nanobots?

"Thanks for the info, CPU," Justin said abruptly. He got up to leave. "Bikes, later?"

CPU closed the laptop and said, " I have to work tonight, maybe next time."

Derrick promised to be there, around two o'clock.

****

A thick wooded area began where the Thymes' backyard ended, with a perfect two-mile path for racing. The two competitors would be able to release some pent-up energy. Derrick was still the champion at climbing trees, long-distance runs, and acorn fights. Justin hoped his new mountain bike would improve his competitive edge.

"Last one to the old tree buys the next pizza," Derrick shouted. He was off like a shot before Justin realized what happened.

Derrick had a good thirty-foot lead over Justin, who was getting tired of shelling out money for pizzas.

"You could give a guy some warning next time," Justin called from behind, pumping as hard as he could.

"Not when pizza is involved," Derrick laughed.

Surrounded by trees and the rustle of leaves, the two bikers wove their way across the bumpy terrain.

A quick glance over his shoulder told Derrick that Justin was now a hundred feet behind him. He smiled.

Suddenly, he heard a sound on his right - the whirring of spokes cutting through the air. The sound grew louder, faster.

"Hey!" Derrick yelled.

Justin suddenly flashed past him, taking a significant lead. Leaves and twigs flew past Derrick's head as he heard Justin call back to him, "I like mushrooms on mine."

Twenty feet separated the two bikers, then thirty, then forty. Just yards from the finish line, Justin's front wheel twisted and he went flying head first over the handlebars. He landed on his knees, crashing down hard on some large rocks.

Derrick was puffing hard when he pulled up alongside him. "Man, that was something."

"I lost it on those rocks," Justin said as he brushed his jeans off.

"I mean, the way you passed me back there. How'd you do that?"

Justin looked down at his jeans. "Oh, look at this. I've blown out the knees on these things and they were new."

"Doesn't that hurt?" Derrick asked.

"I'm fine, but these jeans...."

"You shouldn't be standing given how fast you were going. Look, you're not even bleeding."

"I'm fine," Justin put his hands on his knees and did a few squats, then stood upright. "You're right, I'm not hurt at all."

On the much more subdued ride back to Justin's house, Derrick, so impressed by what had happened, offered to buy two pizzas. Even though, as he was quick to point out, he had won the race on a technicality.

"That's big of you," Justin said.

"I made it to the finish line...you didn't," Derrick reminded him.

"Well, thanks. Just don't forget the mushrooms."

Justin was quiet. Other things were happening to him that, as his father mentioned, had nothing to do with nanobots. They were things that both amazed and frightened him.

What would happen if these powers took control of him, if he couldn't handle it all? It would be easy to take advantage of people for personal gain. It's the kind of thing that made a monster out of a normal guy. He needed to become accountable, and that's what friends were for.

First, there was one more thing to test. A little fun with Derrick couldn't hurt.

With their bikes parked outside on the patio, Justin and Derrick took their seats at the kitchen table. Justin reached back to the counter and grabbed an empty plate, which he then put in front of Derrick. Then he concentrated on the plate and on Derrick.

"Oreos, my favorite." Derrick reached for a handful of invisible cookies and, used to making himself at home, jumped up, found a glass, and poured himself a tall glass of milk.

Justin watched him closely, still concentrating his thoughts on Derrick and the empty plate.

"What happened to the cookies?" Derrick said, shocked to see only crumbs on the plate. "You ate them all?"

Justin got up and found a real bag of Oreos and poured them onto the plate. "Sorry, guess I was hungry. Here you go."

It had worked. Somehow, he was able to get inside Derrick's head and made him see what he wanted him to see. Something like this happened when he first looked into Dawn's eyes. Reaching into someone's mind had caught him by surprise the first time, but he was learning to control the influx of thoughts and feelings. The eyes were his gateway into the essence of a person's character.

A while later, he realized ideas and thoughts could travel both ways. Not only could he see inside someone, he could make them see what was outside their minds as well. It seemed to work best as a defense mechanism, a way to gauge whether someone was friend or foe.

He just needed to know the person's location and be within a couple of hundred yards of them. This test had confirmed it.

Whatever abnormalities his genes carried, the potential benefits of these new abilities did not entirely escape him. In addition, his hearing, memory, sight - all of his senses - were increasing. That much, at least, felt good.

"Derrick, it's time to let you in on a little secret. "

****

Once the two boys met up with CPU at Hi Tech, they sat at their regular booth and Justin explained everything. Derrick, however, wanted some proof, when he noticed Dawn over in the showroom.

"See if you can get more information out of your dad's assistant," Derrick insisted.

Justin was considering the idea when, at that moment, Dawn noticed them sitting by the soda machine. Now she was coming over toward them.

"Hi, guys! You feeling better, Justin?" she asked. Her warm smile melted his heart and he felt his knees weaken. It was good he was sitting down.

"I feel great!" he said, trying to keep his composure. "Join us for a while?" He offered her a seat next to his.

Dawn consented and when her eyes met Justin's, he concentrated and worked his mental magic. It was different this time.

The experience broadened from the last time. He was able to hold a conversation with Dawn on one level and simultaneously analyze her on another. It felt like being two people in one, with two minds. It prevented him from zoning out: he was sure Dawn would never speak to him again if he looked like he'd lost interest in their conversation.

CPU later likened him to a dual-core processor. Then he explained to Justin what that was, of course.

"What part of the planet are you from, Dawn?" Justin asked.

Dawn took the soda Derrick offered her. "Pennsylvania Dutch Country. I have relatives who ride a horse and buggy."

"I thought that's where you were from," CPU said. "You sound different."

"I've never noticed."

"You say stuff like, "Come on over, once," and "Sit awhile," and "What for soda are you drinking? Or, "You're new around here, not?" CPU's wide grin made his eyeglasses slide down his nose.

"Oh, so I talk funny, is that it?" Dawn laughed. "Well, guilty as charged."

"Not," CPU said.

"Did you live on a farm?" Derrick asked.

"Not me. I'm allergic to farms. I'm strictly a city girl, Philadelphia most recently. Left Lancaster, studied science and stayed as far away from farm animals as I could. I was scared by a cow when I was three."

"So, what's it like working for my dad?" Justin asked.

Dawn's cheerful demeanor suddenly turned less enthusiastic. "Your dad is great, but lately it's been rough."

"I'll bet you've been under the gun since the lab was broken into," Derrick said.

"I'll say so, but since that man in security died, they haven't bothered with me much. But it's a frightening thought that a murderer is still at large inside GenEx."

"You're not working today?" Justin asked.

"You're not in school?"

"We graduated last week, me and Derrick," Justin said.

"Oh, right. Well, they closed my department for a few days, pending further investigation into this mess," she explained.

After finishing her soda, Dawn excused herself -something about doing laundry, hair, or both. But before she left she asked, "Justin, since I'm new here, would you mind showing me around Angel Falls? Maybe we could meet at that Red Lobster in town?"

Justin was stunned, but his smile was immediate. "Tonight?"

"Sure, why not?"

"Great! Besides, it will get my mind off a job interview I have coming up."

"You have a job interview?"

"Angel Falls Tribune, next week." Justin wondered if this was an official date, or just two friends hanging out.

"See you later tonight then, Justin," Dawn rose and touched him on the shoulder. "It'll be fun!"

The boys watched her exit, get into a red Cabriolet, and drive away. They huddled closer to Justin.

"What'd you do? Put it into her head that she was talking to Brad Pitt?" Derrick asked him.

CPU laughed, but Justin just ignored the comment and sipped his soda thoughtfully.

"Well, what was she really thinking? Or were you too love-struck to concentrate?" Derrick wanted to know.

Justin's thoughts turned from his date tonight to Derrick's questions and his mood plummeted like a broken elevator. "Something's not right," he said. "Something was blocking me, keeping me out."

"Sounds like love to me," CPU said.

"I couldn't read her, exactly. But she was definitely never scared by a cow," Justin said.

"Anything else?" Derrick asked.

"Interference or maybe it was just confusion. She's definitely afraid of something.

Death - death was an underlying impression, a death in the family, afraid of death...I couldn't tell."

"Maybe she killed someone," CPU said.

"Charles, you're deranged. Maybe she lost a pet," Derrick said. "If Justin likes her, she's OK by me."

"It's all very suspicious," CPU said. "Why would she lie? Are you sure you still want to go out with her?"

"Sure, why not?"

"She's mixed up and you don't really know her. Maybe she's involved with the problems at GenEx - even if Derrick does think I'm deranged. Are you sure you want to get involved?"

"Why not? I like her. But..."

"But?" Derrick and CPU said in unison.

"She does seem to be hiding something."

Chapter 9

The local Red Lobster was nestled in the midst of gift and specialty shops in Falls Square. Every shop entrance opened on to the quaint, streetlamp-lined sidewalks framed by hanging flower baskets. Long shadows cast by a twilight sun created a romantic, mid-summer atmosphere. As tourists rambled about to find the best deals in pottery, home décor, and crafts, Justin made his way to the restaurant.

Dawn was waiting outside. When she saw him, she waved and called to him. He increased his pace. When he reached her side, she locked her arm in his and pulled him close.

"Let's just walk awhile. I'm not hungry yet," she said.

This was just the thing Justin needed, a real stress reliever. Through one store window, they watched a miniature train make its way across a tiny landscape.

"Have you always lived in Angel Falls?" Dawn asked.

"Forever."

"It's nice here. Not as many farms as I'm used to, but slow paced, like home."

"We don't have any horse and buggies here," Justin said.

Dawn laughed. Her laughter rang like a delicate wind chime, light and airy. Her ability to hold a conversation was refreshing, which took even more pressure off him. Coming up with things to talk about tended to be difficult. Her easy charm and soft voice melted away his usual self-consciousness around girls.

As they walked past a shop specializing in all kinds of kites, an ice cream vendor pushed his cart towards them.

"Hungry enough for a cone?" Justin asked.

"Sure!"

The only downside to the cone purchase was releasing Dawn's arm to pay for it. The warmth of her arm in his felt good.

Justin handed Dawn the ice cream. When she took it, she immediately reached for his arm again. They continued their casual stroll past a bookstore, sub sandwich shop and old-fashioned candy store.

Around another corner, an ornate wrought iron and wooden bench invited them sit and watch the sun set beyond the distant plateau. Dawn still held his arm as they took a seat.

"What kind of job are you hoping to get with the paper?" She leaned into Justin, resting her head on his shoulder as she gazed out toward the sunset. Justin was content just to look into her eyes. He'd seen Angel Falls sunsets before. Dawn's eyes were more interesting; her face was like an angel's.

"Photographer for Dr. Siffer's campaign-related functions."

Dawn looked at him curiously. "Not following in your father's footsteps? I'll bet you inherited his smarts. He's quite a brain."

"I've always loved photography. Besides, I'm adopted."

"I never knew that. Even so, it doesn't mean you're not as smart as your dad. I never knew my parents, my uncle raised me." She laid her head back on his shoulder.

Justin would never have called himself smart. But when Dawn compared his intelligence to someone he considered one of the smartest people on earth, he suddenly had to smile. It was a private joke that only he got. The developing power of his mind, the realization that he could learn anything now, struck him as funny. Information was a powerful thing and he had acquired a huge share of it over the last few days.

Derrick was always saying that brain smarts was not as important as spiritual wisdom.

Somehow, when he had said it lately, he seemed to imply that Justin lacked wisdom. Maybe he was jealous, since Derrick had been a little remote recently. CPU never got caught up in the argument, fortunately. Perhaps, if CPU were older…

They sat in silence for several minutes.

Dawn lifted her head off his shoulder and looked directly at Justin. "What's on your mind?" she asked. "You've drifted off."

"Things have been rough, lately. Tonight's been different, nice."

"It is nice," she said, looking out to the horizon. "That's such a pretty view; I'd love to see the waterfall close-up someday."

"What about Saturday? I know a special spot at the top of the falls."

"I'd love to!" Dawn sat up suddenly, "What time is it?"

"Nine-thirty. Why?"

"That late? I have to go." She rose to leave.

"But what about dinner?"

"How about Saturday, after the waterfall?"

They decided she would meet at Justin's and take his car from there.

Dawn apologized for missing dinner, "You were so charming I lost all track of time. It was sweet of you to spend it with me." She kissed him lightly on the cheek and abruptly made a beeline for her car.

"Can I walk you to your car?" Justin called after her.

"That's OK, I'm running late," she said. "See you Saturday."

Justin watched her until she disappeared into the parking lot. Her scent lingered, but the sensation of her kiss began to fade. He wished that moment could have lasted forever.

Making his way to the far end of the lot he let out a deep sigh. Love seemed like a strong word to describe feelings for someone he'd met only days ago. Yet that word kept going through his mind.

The day had been perfect.

Still, it bothered him. Dawn's eyes had told him nothing concrete while they had talked this evening. Fleeting impressions came and went, but only revealed one sure thing: she had lied.

Still, at the core of Justin's being lingered a strange uneasiness unrelated to Dawn's lies. It grew stronger with each step he took. Why was this end of the parking lot so much darker?

An eerie quiet descended upon the area where he stood. The sun had set and a few cars still dotted the mostly empty lot, but he couldn't remember where he parked his car. Something was not right.

The next instant, his brain felt like it was on fire.

Justin grabbed his head and screamed through the searing pain.

But the pain vanished as suddenly as it started. Now he felt unusually alert and noticed several broken overhead lights. Glass was scattered all over the pavement. His head only tingled now, although his thought processes raced with computer speed. Justin calculated, surmised, and then suddenly knew.

These lights had been broken very recently.

He looked around. Had the parking lot changed? His surroundings moved and fluctuated as if being focused through a camera lens. But he didn't have his camera. Everything came into such sharp focus he almost fell forward. He saw every pebble, every crack in the pavement. He didn't just see, he sensed, knowing intimately everything around him. Shadows became lighter and lighted areas brightened. Subtle shades of color now became more brilliant, bolder.

Justin's mind registered "Trouble."

"Hey, geek," a gruff voice growled from behind.

Justin spun around. Three hulks appeared right on top of him.

"Give us your wallet, punk!" spat the man closest to him, his face twisted into a snarl. Before Justin could protest, a tire iron shot through the air toward his head.

Instinctively, Justin's arm shot up to block the blow.

The tire iron struck his arm hard and stopped dead with a loud *clang*, vibrating violently.

"Ow — jeez!" his assailant howled as the tire iron flew from his hands. It landed on the concrete with another sharp ring.

Justin's arm was unharmed, but the tire iron-wielding hood rubbed his hands vigorously at his sides and snarled at him, "Freak!"

His three assailants looked like they were about to pound him. Justin looked around quickly and spotted his car. Then he remembered the Old Testament story of Lot and an angel's ability to blind would-be attackers.

Blind them. The thought forced its way into his head and guided by some powerful, protective impulse he thrust his right hand, palm open, into their faces and yelled at the top of his voice, "Stop!"

A white flash instantly lit the night from all directions at once. The three thugs fell back, pressing their hands to their eyes in a futile attempt to block out the light. They tried to get back up but bumped heads and groped their way around, unable to see. Their ears buzzed and they shouted curses back and forth at each other. They had been robbed of their hearing as well.

Justin made a break for his car, jumped in, and peeled out of there as fast as he could.

Once safely out on the road, he blended in with the heavy traffic and breathed a sigh of relief.

Mental images of Dawn and the sense of normalcy he felt around her had faded.

What happened back there? That thing that welled up inside him and sprang out like a geyser, where did that come from? The flash of light did what he intended, but when he shouted for them to stop…was that his voice he heard? Something had thundered from deep inside his soul. They weren't just blinded. Something resonated across the valley that had temporarily deafened his attackers.

Chapter 10

The sign on the office door read, 'Beverly Heartstone, Assistant Editor'. The twenty-three year old brunette wore a gray business skirt and jacket with a plain white button-down blouse. She sat at a desk buried in photographs and newsprint.

Certificates, awards, and a diploma hung from the wall to her right, while tennis trophies occupied a table against the wall to her left. Most offices burned fluorescent lights day and night, but hers remained off. She preferred the natural light provided by the large window behind her and only resorted to artificial light when she worked late into the evening.

She didn't know whether she lacked a social life because she often worked late, or if she worked late because of her poor social life. Although quite pretty, Beverly was mature for her age, a definite advantage when she applied for this position. She wanted a career and that's what she spent most of her time pursuing.

Justin approached Beverly's office and hesitated before knocking. He took a deep breath and prepared for the first major test of his abilities. This was more important than the parlor tricks he performed for his friends. In spite of feeling uneasy about what he was about to do, it meant getting a job that would mean almost as much to him as Dawn.

The knock on the door was answered with, "Come on in, it's open," from within.

Beverly's pleasant appearance caught Justin completely off-guard. He had envisioned someone much older to be holding such a senior position within the newspaper. Beverly Heartstone was a lot younger and dressed much better than he had imagined. He nailed the messy desk, though.

"You're Justin Thyme," Beverly said.

"Well, I try to be punctual," Justin said, trying to make a joke.

"No. I mean your name is Justin Thyme." Beverly pointed to a leather chair on the other side of her desk. "Have a seat."

Justin sheepishly sank into the plush chair and prepared his mind for the interview. He was about to dive deep into the soul of this newspaper editor. He couldn't imagine what he'd find there and tried to steady his nerves.

"Don't think a recommendation from Dr. Siffer guarantees a job here. He does not own this paper—and certainly not this office." The blank look on Justin's face forced her to do a double take. "Are you listening to me?" she demanded.

He had not quite made the adjustment in his mind. He heard her, but was in the middle of transitioning at the exact moment she decided to look up. He must have looked like a zombie on Benadryl. "Sorry, yes. Just preparing myself," he explained.

"As I was saying, I run this office and everything that goes into the local section comes through me first."

Justin picked up on something more: Fear...confusion...anger.

Beverly continued, "Do you have any problem taking orders from a woman?"

"No," Justin said.

Anxiety.

"You will work directly with me, no one else. And since you'll be representing the paper, you'll take no action before first passing it by me. Understand?"

"Yes, ma'am." She sure had her issues and seemed determined to put him in his place. But after a while, he began to see past her tough façade. Her tirade was as much for her sake as for his. After laying out a few more ground rules, she switched gears.

"Tell me about yourself. Why do you want to work for this office?"

Every time she asked him a question, she revealed more about herself. Isolation.

"I've been taking pictures since I was seven and writing for a couple of years. I enjoy both. I've always wanted to work for a newspaper."

Beverly bit lightly on the eraser of a pencil. She allowed herself only one nervous habit that she didn't try to hide. "What kind of pictures do you like to take?"

"Landscapes, people - all kinds. I have some great nature shots of the lake."

Beverly smirked, "Ever try to take the sword?"

"I have a few pictures of it."

She clarified, "I mean, did you ever try to remove it from the base of the statue? It's something most guys your age have tried."

"My friend Derrick tried. Couldn't budge it and he's a big guy." The questions struck him as odd and it was clear she was playing with him. He just wasn't sure why.

"You didn't try?"

"If Derrick couldn't move it, I sure wouldn't be able to. May I ask what these questions have to do with the job?"

Beverly cleared her throat. "I like to know what makes a prospective worker tick. You know, to get into his personality. You seem levelheaded. That's a good thing."

"Glad I pass," Justin said.

"One more thing, Justin," Beverly said. "Will this job interfere with your school work?"

Justice...integrity...willful.

"I just graduated." Sensing he'd made a favorable impression on Beverly, he felt a little more at ease. She was a different kind of read then Dawn, a fascinating mixture of optimism and sadness. And, she came through loud and clear.

"You high school graduates get younger looking every year. You're eighteen then?"

"Turned eighteen just last week. I want to work for this paper...for you, Ms. Heartstone. This isn't just some summer job. I want to make it my career."

"Can you overlook things you've heard about me and work objectively?"

Intelligence...self-doubt...uncertainty. The question caught him off-guard, as if she had been reading his thoughts and not the other way around.

Beverly repeated the question, "Well, can you?"

Justin switched gears and stopped reading her. She might be fascinating, but she was exhausting. So full of conflicts and fears and yet he had a strong sense she'd be someone worth getting to know. She would be an honest boss, irritable but fair.

"Yes," Justin finally answered after briefly thinking it over.

Beverly cleared her throat. "Most people answer that question rather glibly. I appreciate that you took some time to think about it and I like your honesty. We should work together just fine. I assume you drive. You have a car?"

"Yes."

"Can you start next Monday?"

Justin's face lit up. "I have the job?"

"I'm willing to give you a try."

Justin thanked her profusely with a vigorous, prolonged handshake.

"Don't get mushy - you're welcome," she said. Beverly actually smiled for just a second. It was a nice smile.

Justin got the rundown on dress code, which ISO film and lenses Beverly preferred, and other essentials of the job. In addition to covering Siffer's campaign, she gave him some other responsibilities, including the coverage of local sporting events.

Justin's first assignment would be a local LPGA tournament. He knew nothing about golf, but knew how to take pictures. Beverly wanted lots of photos, from which she'd pick the best for possible inclusion in the paper. He would receive a film allowance, as well as a lunch stipend, since he would be on the road so often.

Justin glanced at the clippings scattered across Beverly's desk and noticed that they were all about GenEx.

He leaned over her desk to pick up one of the clippings. "This GenEx mess must be keeping you busy," he said.

"That's not something you'll be getting involved with," she replied tersely and snatched the paper out of his hand. "It'll be several more years before you break into major news. And my desk is off-limits!"

"Sorry," he said. "It's just that my dad's involved and he's pretty worked up about it."

Beverly stood up to show Justin to the door. "It would be great if we could help everybody, but that's not what we're here for. We just report the news."

Before she let him out, she handed him a laminated three by four card with his name and some numbers on it. "Your press pass. Always keep it with you. Don't lose it and never give it away."

"Thanks. Looks like my picture goes here." He indicated a box above his name.

"Before you leave the building, have your picture taken in personnel. Then you'll be official."

"At least this'll be good news at home. We could use some."

"Must be rough. But I can tell you that they've finally got the person responsible for Gordon's death. That should take some of the pressure off your father. It'll be in tomorrow's edition."

Justin turned, "Who?"

"Your father's assistant. Dawn Stoltzfus."

Chapter 11

Justin's father was on the phone with Detective Selden.

"Dawn worked with you. I just thought you ought to know," Detective Selden said in a matter of fact tone.

"Thanks for filling me in. It's a little hard to believe, she seemed so..."

"They all do, Dr. Thyme. This wasn't your fault. Things just often aren't what they first appear to be."

Dr. Thyme hung up the phone just as Justin returned from his interview. Noticing the distressed look on his face, his father asked, "Didn't things go well with 'Hardball Heartstone', then?"

Justin plopped down onto the couch. "It's not possible."

"What's not?"

"They've arrested Dawn." Justin looked up, pleading, "We've got to help her."

"There's not much we can do, I'm afraid," his dad said. "I just got off the phone with the arresting officer. The evidence against her is pretty solid."

Justin's father explained what he knew, which amounted to everything Detective Selden had just told him.

Shortly after the vial's disappearance was discovered, Dawn and Gordon were overheard having a heated discussion. The police believed Dawn had stolen the vial, but they were not sure how. An anonymous tip led them to a pair of pliers in Dawn's apartment. Her fingerprints were the only ones on it and the peculiar ridge pattern on the teeth matched the pattern on the loosened bolts from Gordon's railing. That was enough to bring her in for questioning.

"This person who overheard them called it in?" Justin asked.

"Yes. Anonymously."

"That sounds suspicious. They must be hiding something. Why did it take so long to come forward?"

"Whoever it was claimed to have been away on a cruise during that time and didn't even know a crime had been committed until now."

"I've gotten to know her, dad. She couldn't kill anyone."

"She'll have a good lawyer. We'll have to pray that justice will be done."

Justin would pray, but he knew he could do more. And what about Beverly? Deep in the fabric of her being lived a desire to know the truth, to see fair treatment for everyone. If only she and the paper could do something.

But Beverly had been adamant that she wasn't about to change her mind and let him in on this story. They "just report the news", and he wasn't going to jeopardize his working relationship with her before he had even started. Unless - what if he let her in on his secret?

But his circle of confidantes must not get too large. If he made enemies, they would be making enemies too, by association. Endangering his friends was the last thing he wanted to do.

"You were pretty taken by her, huh?" His dad asked.

"We were supposed to meet tomorrow. I guess that won't happen now."

"She's allowed visitors - for the time being."

"Under these circumstances, she probably doesn't want anyone to see her."

"Actually, she asked for you."

"Why didn't you say so?" Up like a shot, Justin headed for the front door. "Be back in a while and oh, I got the job."

His father waved him off, "Good going. Be careful."

****

Twenty minutes later, a thick window of bulletproof glass separated Justin and Dawn. She looked worn out and pale in the drab, gray prison uniform. Still, even under these circumstances, she looked better than any girl he'd ever known. A female guard, arms folded and a perpetual scowl on her face, stood behind Dawn, watching.

"You've got to believe me. I had nothing to do with any of this." Dawn told Justin. She could hardly bring herself to look at him.

"I can help you, Dawn. I have some, uh, resources I can use to make this right. The Tribune has all sorts of information on your case that could be helpful too."

"You got the job?" Dawn smiled and finally looked up. "I knew you would." She reached her hand out to him, but the glass stopped her. "I'm scared..."

"You'll be out of here soon, don't worry."

"Sorry about our trip to the falls."

"We'll get another chance...soon."

When visiting time was over, Justin excused himself and promised he'd find out what really happened. Instead of going straight to his car, he had another idea.

The jail was part of the larger Justice Complex, which included the police station, courthouses, a forensics lab, and a morgue. Mike Gordon's body was being held at the morgue, according to recent news reports, while the investigation was still ongoing. A visit to the morgue might shed some light on what had really happened.

Justin passed the forensics lab. There was no one in the medical examiner's office, so he wandered around the halls until someone stopped him.

"May I help you, young man?" asked a woman wearing a white lab coat. The name, Leslie Graves, stood out in red letters on her lab badge and she noticed Justin reading it. "And no cracks about my name."

"Excuse me?" Justin said, looking puzzled.

"You know, my name's Graves, and I work in a morgue. I try to stay a step ahead of the jokers."

"It hadn't crossed my mind."

"You'd be the first. What can I do for you?"

"I was wondering how things were going with the Gordon case."

Leslie noticed the press pass hanging from a lanyard around Justin's neck. "Is this personal or professional?"

"A little of both. Gordon was a friend of the family; he worked with my father. But the Tribune would like an update too."

"Sure, Justin Thyme - you must be Mark's son. Come on in."

Leslie guided Justin into one of the exam rooms. He immediately realized they were not entirely alone. A body lay stretched out on one of the metal exam tables.

Justin looked away quickly, "That's - is that Mr. Gordon?"

"You were expecting Elvis, maybe? That's him, alright."

The color drained from Justin's face when he saw the dead, cut-up body of Gordon. The smell of formaldehyde filled the air and made him sick.

"Don't worr, we get that reaction a lot. This your first time seeing a dead guy?"

Justin nodded and tried to compose himself. The body could wait. Leslie might have answers to his questions, so he concentrated on getting as much information as he could from her.

"Uh, the cause of death was the fall, right?" he asked.

"You bet. Multiple fractures, paired with some internal bleeding. The broken neck did the trick. He didn't die immediately, but he couldn't have lasted more than a few minutes."

"No other marks on the body?"

"Nothing inconsistent with a twelve-story fall. You must watch a lot of crime shows on TV."

"He was pretty beat up?"

"Concrete's not too gentle."

This wasn't getting anywhere. Justin worked up his courage and peeked back at the body on the exam table. The chest cavity was open, the top of the head missing, as was the brain. Fortunately, he made good use of a nearby sink and threw up in it.

"That's OK. My sink gets a lot of that from visitors," Leslie said.

"Sorry. At least there's nothing left in my stomach for an encore." Justin composed himself again and continued, "Was there anything unusual about his condition?"

"Well, nothing to speak of. I mean, nothing that would lead to any other conclusions, but it was curious,"

"What do you mean?"

"I located a small needle-prick between two toes on his left foot. I checked the area and it was clean. To be sure, I ran blood tests. Everything showed up normal."

"Was he diabetic?"

"Not according to his medical records. My, but you are thorough."

"Do you have an electron microscope?" Justin asked.

"Here? Why would we?"

"Just curious. Thanks for your time. Uh, when is he getting buried?"

"Cremated." Leslie corrected. "Tomorrow."

"I thought the body was being saved for evidence."

"He's told us everything he can. Besides, he's overdue on his rent." Her laugh caught Justin by surprise.

Leslie escorted Justin out of the lab and to the main lobby, toward the ME's office. He thanked her again for talking to him.

There'd be no time to return for evidence later. Something in that exam room would prove Dawn's innocence. Justin was sure of it.

He watched as Leslie entered the ME's office down the hall and closed the door. It was a corner office, all windows and bright light. No one could access the exam room without being seen. Well, almost no one.

Justin concentrated on Leslie as she sat at her desk. He saw her look up and wave to him— except he was walking past her at that moment. She was waving to someone back in the main lobby, someone who wasn't there.

He quickly found the exam room, listening in case anyone was coming. He also made sure he did not look directly at Gordon again. A refrigerator in the corner of the room held several tubes of blood labeled with Gordon's name. He took one, hoping no one would miss it, and rushed back to the main hall and the lobby, carefully hiding the vial inside the pocket of his jeans.

Now all he had to do was touch everyone's mind so he could leave unseen.

A hand grabbed his shoulder.

"You lost, son?" A large security guard looked down at him, at least five inches taller than Justin and twice his size.

"Bathroom?" Justin blurted.

"You'll need to use the one by the main visitor's entrance. Follow me."

The guard took Justin back past Leslie's office. Fortunately, she was no longer there. He showed him the men's room and let him go. Justin went in and hid in one of the stalls to regroup. He counted himself fortunate that no one else had seen him leaving the exam room the second time.

He checked his jeans pocket. The tube of blood was intact and so was he. Holding the bathroom door ajar, he glanced out. No one in sight, including the guard. He prepared for one last set of mind tricks, which he'd pull the second he saw anyone. Then he made a mad dash for the main entrance, just yards away.

By the time Justin got back to the parking garage and found his car, it was getting late. His mind had been so preoccupied with finding a way to examine Gordon's blood he had trouble remembering where he parked. And every level of these parking garages looked the same.

GenEx Lab's electron microscope would be strictly off-limits. Besides, how would he explain to his father that he had swiped evidence from the morgue? As he mulled over his options, two things caught his eye. The first was two stories down in the street below. In the late evening light, it looked like Siffer's limo was pulling away from police headquarters.

The second thing he noticed was a Mercedes parked in a no-parking zone. The vehicle had his car effectively blocked in so it couldn't move. There was no way he'd be able to maneuver around the guy, unless his car was positioned ninety degrees to the left.

Justin muttered angrily under his breath, "Where's the justice? Dawn's in jail, now this bozo gets away with illegal parking."

He grunted in disgust and grabbed the rear bumper of the Mercedes, lifting it three feet off the ground. Without thinking, he swung it ninety degrees to the left and let it drop. Now the Mercedes was wedged into a corner and Justin's car had an opening.

"Let's see you maneuver out of there," he laughed. Then he stepped back and realized what he had done. He looked down at his hands and back to where the car used to be. "Awesome."

Chapter 12

Beverly did not let her face show how amazed she was with Justin's first set of pictures. Of course, she couldn't really hide her thoughts from him. But why not tell him? Maybe this was another control technique.

"I can probably use one or two of these," she said, assuming a tone of indifference. "Use the filter I recommended next time."

Justin played along. "I don't really understand golf. Maybe if you explained the game to me, I'd get better pictures?"

"Uh, what?" She replied, with a caught-off-guard expression. "No, that's not necessary." She tossed the photos onto her desk. "Let's see the campaign shots."

One pose showed Dr. Siffer holding some young children on his knees, revealing an uncharacteristically compassionate side of him. Another showed him assisting an elderly citizen. All the shots demonstrated a caring, concerned leader in action.

"What, no pictures of Siffer throwing someone out of a building or kicking them down the stairs?"

Justin laughed.

Beverly stopped flipping through them and asked, "What's with the telephoto lens?"

"Weird, huh? The photographers were not allowed to get close to him. I did the best I could under the circumstances."

"He's getting paranoid. He'll be posing behind bullet-proof glass next."

Justin wondered what Beverly's politics were and whether she supported Siffer's campaign. It didn't sound like it, but he hadn't heard her say anything of a serious nature about anything except the need to get good pictures. She worked hard not to reveal a personal side.

Based on what he had been able to 'read', Justin figured that Beverly wanted to stay objective. She had told him that her job was to report and that's all. He sensed enough integrity in her to realize that her political beliefs would not influence how she reported on the issues. Still, a glimpse at her personal side would be nice detour occasionally.

"OK for the first attempt," Beverly said, letting this second batch of photos drop unceremoniously onto her already cluttered desk. "Don't forget to be at the press conference tonight and the banquet tomorrow night. They'll provide you with even better photo opportunities."

"Siffer wants to open up the GenEx mess for questions tonight," Justin mentioned, hoping Beverly would volunteer some information about the case.

"I know. I'm sending one of our reporters out. You just get the pictures and that's it. I've already told you this story is off-limits."

"But, my friend..."

"If you're referring to Dawn Stoltzfus, forget it. Stay objective - never get personally involved with the story, or with suspects."

"What if I told you I might have evidence...?"

Beverly looked at him sternly. "What kind of evidence?"

Justin knew she'd fire him if he told her what he had taken from the morgue. There was no way he would risk it.

"Your silence is deafening," she said. She showed him to the door. "Stick to photography and we'll work just fine together."

Once Justin was out in the hallway, Beverly shut the door behind him, harder than usual.

****

Beverly stared out of her window, alone with her thoughts. Angel Falls stretched out lazily below her, with barely a cloud in the sky.

Suddenly, without realizing it, a powerful desire rising from deep inside her became audible.

"I wish someone cared for me the way he cares for that girl."

Embarrassed to realize that she had actually spoken the words out loud, she quickly glanced around her office. Of course, no one was there and no one had heard her. She shrugged it off as a moment of weakness. It wouldn't happen again.

Still in the hallway outside Beverly's door, Justin heard. And he knew what he had to do.

****

Justin drove to CPU's house, Derrick already with him in the back seat. "C'mon, let's go," Justin yelled from the driver-side window.

CPU called out a quick, "Later" to his mom, and ran to the car. He hopped into the back seat next to Derrick and they drove off.

"Why are we going to the University?" CPU asked.

"That science project thing you won last year? We're going to use it," Justin said. "You have the pass with you, don't you?"

"I've never seen our little geek friend without it. I think he sleeps with it," Derrick teased.

"Yeah, it's right here," CPU pulled out his free pass to the University's electron microscope. "And I don't sleep with it." He punched Derrick in the side.

Derrick never felt it, but moved closer to his side of the back seat, pretending to avoid CPU's fist. "Now, if you had a Topps Mickey Mantle from 1952," he said, "I'd understand your excitement."

CPU informed Derrick that only three passes had been awarded that year. Out of eighty eligible students, he was one of the lucky few.

"I need to look at something under the big 'scope, but they can't know what it is," Justin said.

"Like, what's the deal?" Derrick asked.

"It's blood and it has to be our secret. We have to tell them it's something else, like seawater."

"I'm sure they'll know the difference between seawater and-" Derrick stopped suddenly. A look of understanding appeared on his face. "Oh, another disappearing-plate-of-cookies trick, huh?"

"Where'd you get blood? And whose blood is it?" CPU asked.

"Mike Gordon's, from the morgue."

CPU freaked. "You stole blood from the morgue."

"I'll bet I know how you pulled that one off too," Derrick said with an air of smug satisfaction.

"But that's like taking evidence, isn't it?" CPU shouted.

"Relax, I just borrowed it. I'm betting there's a clue here that'll prove Dawn's innocence. I'll bring it back tomorrow, promise."

"An electron microscope...are you thinking nanobots?" CPU asked.

"Right. And I'm betting these bots were up to no good."

"Who'd do that?" CPU asked.

Derrick jumped in, "Justin, this could backfire. What if Dawn is the thief? She's still the most likely suspect."

"You even said she was hiding something," CPU reminded him.

"Dad says the security tape proves she didn't. Besides, I know she's not a murderer."

Parking at Angel Falls University was plentiful. Except for a few summer students, things were relatively quiet. Public tours of the science department were available year round. Tours included the electron microscope, and the largest planetarium for two hundred miles. This was the perfect time for CPU to use his ticket.

Justin gave them instructions before they presented the guest pass. "CPU, tell them you want to look at some seawater under the 'scope. Tell them to get the sample from me, and when I hand them the tube, play along with whatever they say. Derrick, don't you say anything."

Inside the University, an older man dressed in a rumpled blue suit and tie received them in the large room that housed the microscope. He introduced himself as Dr. Ralph Boyer, professor of biology. The only other person in the room, a technician, monitored several computer screens. A large box stood off to one side with an equally large cylindrical tube running through it. Heavy cables connected the cylinder and tube to something shaped like a large trash can. Another bank of controls, adjacent to the computers, were lit up like a Christmas tree.

Dr. Boyer motioned to CPU and said, "Henry, this young man has a sample of seawater for us to study."

Henry rose from his control seat and approached CPU, but CPU pointed to Justin, "He has it."

"I'll need to prepare it," Henry looked from CPU to Justin, who carefully handed him the test tube.

For the first time in his life, Derrick actually kept quiet.

Justin penetrated the minds of Dr. Boyer and Henry. Somewhere, in a deeper part of his mind, Justin thought of seawater and reached into that deep area of their minds, made contact, and became one with their thoughts.

The prepared sample of blood entered the scope. Justin signaled his friends to stand next to him.

"We need to be quiet," he whispered to Derrick and CPU. "Respond to what they respond to. Follow their lead."

"I'd direct your attention to the large-screen monitor on the wall over there," Dr. Boyer said. "Your sample is coming into focus now."

The three boys stood watching, awestruck. Dozens of ciliated mechanical spheres swirled and darted back and forth on the large screen in front of them. They moved as if they were alive, full of purpose and design, and bent on performing a task that remained hidden—except to the one who programmed them.

But these things were not hidden from Justin.

Seeing them for the first time sent a tingle down the back of his neck. They looked like living things, not robots. He wondered if the nanobots inside him were aware of the ones on the screen, if they could communicate with each other.

"Quite an interesting sample, young man," Dr. Boyer said.

All three boys took a deep breath simultaneously.

"An excellent sample of parameoba eilhardi. This amoeba is known to cause disease in blue crabs. It's very interesting."

CPU looked at Justin quizzically and whispered, "How do you know about this amoeba?"

"I don't; he does. I'm just suggesting seawater and his mind fills in the blanks. I think he sees what he wants to."

"Awesome," Derrick whispered.

Dark areas dotted the silvery surface of the bots, a view of the miraculously small inner workings. As Dr. Boyer droned on about picoplankton, Justin's attention focused on the occasional bursts of light emanating randomly from the nanobots. It made him uncomfortable.

"Dr. Boyer, we should be returning our sample back to school soon," Justin said anxiously.

"Truly remarkable. Tell your school I said thank you for letting you bring it in today."

Henry removed the sample from the scope, cleaned up his equipment, and handed the test tube back to Justin. After some final handshakes and goodbyes, the boys walked back to Justin's car.

"That was amazing," CPU shouted.

"Weird," Derrick added.

"They were sending out electric shocks," Justin said. "Did you notice that?"

"I saw it too," Derrick said. "Like lightning flashes."

"What would that feel like inside your head?" CPU asked.

"I don't know, but I think it sent Gordon over the edge." Justin answered.

"So, now what?" CPU asked.

"I'm going to cover a press conference tonight, right after I get this sample back to the morgue."

"Then what?" Derrick asked.

"Then, we're going to get inside Mike Gordon's apartment and have a look around."

Chapter 13

Justin eased into his customary plush chair in Beverly's office and began to daydream out her window while she examined his latest photographic efforts. He had taken a routine press conference and transformed it into an incredible photo essay.

"The pictures are pretty good," Beverly admitted to him. At least it was something. "I see they kept the press at a distance again."

Justin shook off the creeping stupor and sat up. "Derrick says it's because Siffer's up to no good."

"Who's Derrick?"

"A friend. He doesn't trust politicians, especially Siffer."

"I know the type. That kind of thinking, the lack of objectivity, wouldn't work here, but you already know that."

"But as a reporter, how fishy do things have to get before you start to connect the conspiracy dots?"

"If you're referring to the GenEx case, what's the connection with this candidate?"

"None that I can see - yet. But there's more to GenEx's problems than even the coroner's office knows," Justin said. He immediately wished he hadn't.

Beverly tossed his pictures aside and came down forcefully with both hands on her desk, leaning right into his face.

Justin lurched back in his seat.

"What have you been up to?" she demanded. "How is it you think you know something the coroner doesn't?"

"I have a theory..."

"Who doesn't?"

"Gordon was murdered, even if he threw himself off that balcony."

"What you've described is, by definition, a suicide." Beverly stepped back and began to pace behind her desk.

"The coroner found a needle mark between Gordon's toes."

"The coroner! You went to the coroner?" She stopped pacing for a second to glare at him. "You're still trying to save your girlfriend, even though I told you not to become involved?"

"Someone injected him with something."

"How do you-"

"Nanobots in his blood. I saw them. It's what drove him off that balcony. I'm sure of it."

"You saw them?"

"Under an electron microscope."

Justin saw something like a light suddenly flash in Beverly's eyes as she made the connection. Her expression went from anger to surprise. She became calmer, in spite of herself. "The vial stolen from GenEx Labs..."

"Someone programmed them to attack Gordon's nervous system." Justin said. "Gordon had the security tapes. He knew something he wasn't supposed to."

Beverly sank thoughtfully into her chair. Justin's theory sounded more like science fiction, but given the events of the past two weeks, anything was possible.

"First," she said, "your girlfriend was released on bail yesterday. If you're right, it does seem unlikely that an eighteen-year-old could have masterminded something of this magnitude. Second, the coroner never released such information. How did you come by it?"

Justin described, in as few details as possible, his trip to the Medical Examiner's office and the electron microscopy lab at Angel Falls University.

"That doesn't explain..."

"I told you I could help."

"You didn't answer my question."

"It's a long story," Justin said.

"I'm a newspaper editor, I like stories. What gives?"

Now that he had backed himself into the proverbial corner, he had to tell her. She was trustworthy; he knew that from the first time he looked into her eyes. Having worked with her, he was even more certain of it.

Justin bared his soul to Beverly, explaining everything in vivid detail. The visions, the meeting with Mr. Hardy, even his run-in with the three delinquents at Falls Square. He left nothing out. Beverly listened, but her incredulous expression told Justin she wasn't buying his story.

After a half hour, she interrupted, "I said I liked stories, but I never cared for science fiction."

"I'll prove it. In ten seconds, you'll hear a knock on the door. When it opens, you'll believe me."

"In about ten seconds you'll no longer be employed by this newspaper." Beverly stood, leaned over her desk and glared at him again. "Hand over your press pass," she demanded.

There was a knock on her door.

"Answer it," Justin told her.

Beverly eyed him curiously and tentatively called, "Come in."

The door opened and, out in the hall, stood Justin, smiling back at her. She looked down at the first Justin, still sitting in the chair across from her.

Her jaw dropped as she felt behind her for her chair and collapsed into it.

"Stop it," Beverly yelled.

Immediately, the door closed and things in the office went back as they were a moment earlier. The door had never actually opened. Only one Justin sat across from her now.

"Sorry," he said. "I didn't know it would have that effect on you."

"I told my sister she was an 'angel' once. It was just an expression. I didn't think they were real."

"I'm not sure I did, either. Derrick's been bugging me about it."

"He sounds like a good friend..."

Chapter 14

Senator Roland Williams refused to take any calls. Party members from every corner of the nation kept his phone ringing off the hook. He did not have to answer to them. He would back Siffer's campaign and that was that.

Isolated in his office, sweat beading on his brow, his fingers fumbled with the Advil bottle. It dropped to his desk, unopened. He angrily grabbed it up and twisted the top, sending dozens of small brown pills flying across the floor.

He cursed the inventor of the safety cap and threw the empty plastic bottle against the wall.

"Governor Cahill is on the line, Senator," his secretary's voice pierced his temples. He thought he had turned down the volume on that blasted intercom.

Wilson grabbed his temples and shouted at the machine, "I'm not in. I'm not in."

He would back Siffer. He told himself that repeatedly during the past few days, since first announcing it to the press. Why? He suppressed the question each time it came up, which was often. He could not come up with an answer.

He would back Siffer. Tonight, at the banquet, he would give a speech. Sing the praises of Siffer. Why?

He must, that's why.

****

Justin, Derrick, and CPU waited by the entrance of the Falls View Apartments. The security doors were always locked and they didn't know anyone who could buzz them in. They'd been waiting twenty minutes for someone to leave so they could sneak in behind them before the door closed again.

"Your dad and mom are invited?" Justin asked Derrick.

"Sure. He's invited all the small business owners," Derrick boasted. His father owned the largest auto parts and repair center in Angel Falls. "I get to go too."

"How does that make you feel, knowing you can't stand Siffer?" Justin jabbed.

"Free food is free food." Derrick smiled. "That's all I'm going for. The dinner's supposed to be outstanding!"

"My dad's going too," CPU said. "He's seen the menu. I wish I could go, but I'm not old enough to vote."

"I'm not persuaded either way yet," Justin said. "I'm only there for the pictures."

"People are getting hot over this election," CPU said. "There've been fights breaking out across the entire state."

"I know," Derrick said. "A small riot erupted outside the movie theater last night."

"I heard that after the movie, some guy got jumped just because of his campaign button," Justin said.

CPU tugged Justin's arm and whispered, "Someone's coming out. How will we get past the guy at the security desk?"

"Leave that to me," Justin reassured him.

The three boys grabbed the door just before it latched shut and entered the building. Justin motioned them to stay close and quiet. Under his influence, they slipped past a uniformed guard who was watching television. Derrick knew what Justin was doing with the guard's mind. He made a face at the guard and waved to him as they passed.

As soon as they turned the corner and got out of sight, Justin gave Derrick a light punch in the shoulder. "Knock it off. I almost started laughing and I need to concentrate."

They took the elevator to the twelfth floor and found Gordon's apartment. Police Crime Scene tape stretched across the door, but there was no one standing guard outside.

"How're we getting in?" CPU asked.

Justin groaned and collapsed against the door. "Some plan. Of course it's locked."

CPU's face lit up. "If an angel can appear anywhere, why can't you?"

"Yeah, transport yourself inside, unlock the door, and let us in," Derrick said with a big, toothy grin.

Justin was getting frustrated. "That's like, totally crazy."

"No crazier than the other stuff we've seen you do," CPU reminded him.

Justin considered the point. His whole life had taken on a surreal quality. Who knows? What was one more strange thing added to his life.

He faced the door and closed his eyes. Now what? He tried to imagine what was on the other side of the door.

Nothing.

He pushed against the door as if to squeeze through the pores in the wood, being glad it wasn't a metal door.

Nothing.

He leaned back and then let himself fall into the door.

"Ouch!" Nothing except for a bruised shoulder.

Eyes closed, he raised his hands and tried to imagine the inside of the room again, this time pretending the door was not there.

Let's go inside.

A vision suddenly appeared in his mind. It was an apartment room in need of cleaning. Items were strewn about the floor and furniture. He moved his feet and heard the rustle of newspaper.

Muffled sounds of excitement seemed to come from behind him. He opened his eyes and turned around to find himself facing the door from the inside. The excited sounds came from his friends on the outside. The rustling was a newspaper he was standing on.

He opened the door and let them in.

"Shh! Let's not attract too much attention, OK?"

"That was awesome!" CPU said. "One second you're here, and the next you're gone!"

"Hurry up, come in," Justin urged. He quickly shut the door behind them. The place was a mess with newspapers scattered everywhere and books knocked off their shelves. The only area that looked untouched was the bedroom, as if Gordon hadn't slept there for days prior to his death.

"Sleep deprivation would cause someone to jump off a balcony," CPU said.

"Maybe the nanobots kept him awake," Derrick reminded him.

CPU thought about it. "And made him open to suggestions."

"Or controlled him completely," Justin said. "Let's spread out and look around."

They had no idea what to look for, so they searched for anything out of the ordinary.

Gordon had a decent DVD collection that included old and new movies, including some classic science fiction, which impressed CPU. His setup was standard: a twenty-seven-inch television, DVD player, and a set of external speakers that all fitted nicely in an oak multimedia cabinet.

Something caught Justin's attention.

The video player seemed out of place, sitting on a shelf by itself. The wires weren't hidden, like the rest of the stereo equipment, but ran across the top of some books to the back of the television. Justin didn't remember seeing any VHS tapes in the entire apartment.

Unless...He hit the eject button on the VCR. Sure enough, out popped a tape and he held it up. "Look!"

Derrick grabbed it and read the label. "It's blank. But why would someone with a DVD collection have just one video tape?"

"Maybe he recorded something on it," CPU said.

Justin grabbed the tape and popped it back into the player. "Let's see."

CPU turned on the TV and Justin pressed play. He immediately recognized Dawn in the center of the picture. The time and date of the recording flashed and scrolled across the four corners of the image. They could not decipher the other information, but it was familiar to Justin.

"It's a copy of the security information from GenEx," Justin realized.

"Isn't that, like, illegal or something?" Derrick asked.

"Or something, yes," Justin said. "It's the tape that proves Dawn didn't steal the nanobots."

"Why would Gordon need this? Didn't he already watch it with your dad and Siffer?" Derrick asked.

"Two days before Gordon died."

"Why would he risk losing his job for this? Are you sure about what's on it?" CPU asked.

"Well, there's one way to find out." Justin ejected the tape back out of the VCR. "We need to get out of here. I'll watch this at home."

****

An elegant dining hall, filled with two hundred and fifty guests, was not where Justin preferred to be right now. Meeting Dawn later at the falls was all he wanted to do. But a job was a job. Meanwhile, he'd try to concentrate on getting through this assignment.

Dr. Siffer had spared no expense. A live orchestra played old people tunes in that 'easy listening' style that sounded like elevator music. Towering over everything in the center of the hall, an enormous ice sculpture glistened, flowing with a great waterfall of sparkling punch.

127

These folks must be thirsty if the line around the hulking chunk of ice was any indication. Justin wasn't hungry. And he didn't like sherbet, a key ingredient of the punch, so that did not interest him either. His mission: get pictures and see Dawn. He moved through the crowd. A few prominent and influential residents reluctantly posed for him. Many of them admitted that they did not agree with Siffer's politics while some sat on the fence. Apparently, like Derrick, none of them could turn down free food. Justin even got a shot of Derrick at the punch bowl.

A large movie screen hung center-stage above a podium. Long curtains closed off the rest of the stage behind it. The curtains began to rustle and a small man appeared from behind them. He approached the podium and, on cue, the orchestra fell silent. The little man requested that everyone take a seat. He then introduced Senator Roland Williams.

Senator Williams entered from stage left, his gait hesitant, like someone finding his way in the dark. The senator's face appeared sickly pale through Justin's zoom lens. When the senator spoke, his words were slurred. He spoke of Siffer's accomplishments almost mechanically, like a recorded message, and frequently wiped his brow with a handkerchief. Some emergency prevented Dr. Siffer from appearing in person, so the senator directed everyone's attention to the screen overhead.

Williams introduced Siffer before making his way backstage. On the screen, larger than life, the doctor's image appeared from a book-filled study. He stood in front of a large leather chair behind an ornate mahogany desk, on which he rested his trademark panama hat, cape, and walking stick. Then he took a seat.

"Thank you for coming tonight," Siffer began. "I want to extend my support to you, the area's business owners. I hope you will consider electing me as your governor. Your entrepreneurial skills have put Angel Falls on the map. My election will ensure our continued growth and your prosperity. Please, help yourselves to campaign material and enjoy the meal. Try some punch - and have a good evening."

The screen went blank and the orchestra started playing again, softly.

Derrick approached Justin, who sat in a corner, loading a new roll of film into his camera. "This punch is great. Have some?"

"No, I'm just about done here. Next stop, Dawn and Visitation Lake."

"It's a good thing Siffer's speech was short and sweet. The food's really good."

"Did you notice the Senator?" Justin asked.

"Yeah. Maybe he has the flu."

"It's not flu season." Justin secured the back of the camera and closed the exposed roll inside the camera bag. "Well, Derrick, I'm outta here. Enjoy your dinner."

"Later," Derrick called, but Justin had already disappeared into the crowd.

On the way back to his table, Derrick suddenly had to steady himself. An odd feeling hit him between the eyes and he felt overwhelmingly dizzy. He staggered and dropped into his seat. Falling forward, he hit his head on the table.

He was out cold.

Chapter 15

An unseasonably cool breeze swept across the lake. Justin was glad he had brought a jacket. He offered it to Dawn. She had arrived at the lake about five minutes after he did. She accepted it with a shiver and they found a place to sit beneath the willow tree.

"I like this," she said. She huddled a little closer.

"Better when it's not so chilly," Justin's teeth chattered, although probably more from nerves than the cool air.

"Put your arm around me if you're cold," Dawn said.

Thankfully, she broke the ice by offering her shoulder.

"Do you miss Pennsylvania?" he asked.

"Not really. I've met some real nice people here." She gave him a quick glance and smiled. "I have a good job, a nice place to live."

"What about your family?" Justin watched her look out across the lake. He loved to watch her expressions, her movements. It was something he could do it for hours. Now, suddenly, she seemed distant, as far away as the home she had left.

"I don't have much family left. My mother left me with her brother when my father died. She couldn't handle raising a kid by herself. I haven't seen her since I was ten."

"I never met my biological mother. I'm curious about her."

"No brothers or sisters?" she asked.

"Nope. None that I know of, anyway."

With an impish look Dawn asked, "You're one of those bratty, 'only child' types?"

"No way!" Justin gave her shoulder a gentle jostle and smiled. "I'm a model son."

Dawn looked into his eyes for a second and then quickly looked back towards the lake. Her smile faded. "I wish I could say I was a model daughter."

The sun rested low on the horizon, creating an orange-red luster. On the far horizon, darkness was closing in. Justin opened up to Dawn about his hopes and dreams while she sat and listened. She fell quiet during the course of the conversation. He sensed conflicting emotions boiling up inside her. But there was a sudden vagueness in her manner that prevented him from reading anything specific. He had no idea what could have caused her mood to drop so suddenly.

Justin was reminiscing about growing up with his two best friends when he noticed a tear form in the corner of her eye.

"You're a sweet guy, Justin," she began. "Being with you helps me to forget about my life, like things really could be different."

Another tear began to fall.

Justin held her a little closer, wiped her tears, and said, "Being with you has been good for me too."

He leaned in, daring to give her a kiss, when she quickly stood up. "Don't, Justin,"she said, wiping her eyes. "I'm sorry but you're better off not getting too involved with me."

Before he knew what had happened, she ran to her car and drove away. He didn't bother to call her back. He could tell it would be pointless.

Twenty minutes later, Justin was still sitting in the same spot under the willow tree, in the dark.

What happened here?

It was late and thinking was tiresome. On the way to his car, he passed the odd monument, more noticeable now that someone had cleared away some of the weeds. The inscription on the plaque was barely readable in the diminishing light.

When he passed his hand over the coarse, weathered chair, he felt something tremble, a low rumble that approached from the distance, growing in intensity. The wind shifted abruptly, violently, hitting him hard in the face. He gripped the chair to steady his footing.

The rumble became a high-pitched whine. The monument vibrated and hummed under his touch. The wind, whipped to frenzy, assaulted him with debris from every direction.

Then the vision returned. The same one he knew from before, only now he controlled it. He could slow the scenes and focus on shapes, though the faces still remained obscure.

The wind howled and grew even more volatile. Lightning streaked across the sky. Billowing black clouds rapidly closed in on the plateau. Justin's hands moved up the monument and the vision continued. Lightning flashed. It hit the ground just yards away.

What earlier appeared as a flowing, ghostly apparition now became a large man.The flowing thing was a cloak or cape floating behind him.

The wind screamed.

Justin's hands passed over the golden sword. Where flesh met metal, the weapon glowed with a searing white light. Suddenly, an intense ray of light split the darkness, propelling Justin twenty feet in the air. The vision stopped.

Justin found himself flat on his back, looking up at the stars.

It was dead calm.

****

Justin arrived home after eleven, feeling part tired and part wired with the adrenalin still pumping through his system. Sleep would be impossible. The day's events echoed repeatedly in his mind: the security video, the dinner, and Dawn's weird behavior.

Most unusual was what happened after Dawn left. There was a presence, an ominous force, in the windstorm. Something, or someone, was out to get him. Or he was just crazy after all.

Touching the sword prompted the vision's return. Was the power in the sword, him, or both? One thing seemed certain: holding on to it protected him from the vicious windstorm.

Suddenly, like a punch to the head, the connection hit his tired brain. The sword had responded to his Nephilim gene. In that moment all doubts about who or what he was vanished. What it meant in the larger scheme of things was not yet clear.

Dawn's behavior was another mystery he couldn't fathom. If he got the chance, he'd try to talk to her later. But at the moment, the image of the caped man was too disturbing to think about anything else.

The videotape.

Since he couldn't sleep, he grabbed the tape and put it into their VCR. This could be a waste of time, but there had to be something in it that caused

Gordon to lose his life. If it was there, he wanted to find it.

The tape played on for forty-five minutes, revealing nothing out of the ordinary. Security must be a boring occupation, but he enjoyed seeing Dawn work. The information blinking in the corners of the TV screen was about to cure his insomnia.

A robot arm moved the vial. Dawn wrote notes on a pad. She typed more information into her computer. Equipment in the lab blinked with the colors of multiple LEDs. Dawn dropped the vial of nanobots into her lab coat.

Into her lab coat! Justin was suddenly shocked back into an adrenalized state. It was so blatantly obvious, how did anyone miss this? She took the vial from the lab. But how did she get the vial past security and out the front door?

Justin's shock suddenly turned into fear and sadness. Dawn was guilty.

****

"What's so important that it can't wait till morning?" Justin's dad asked. "What's this?"

Justin handed him the videotape. "You should see this," he said. "We found it in Gordon's apartment."

"What were you doing in Gordon's apartment?"

"Looking for evidence and here it is. You have to see it."

His dad pushed the 'play' button. As soon as he saw what kind of information was on it, he quickly pulled it out to examine it. This tape certainly was not official GenEx material, but what was on it looked official.

His dad was incredulous. "You got this at Gordon's apartment?"

"Earlier today."

"This can't be!" His dad shoved the tape back into the VCR and hit 'play' again. "As amazing as the existence of this tape is, it's nothing new; I've already seen this exact thing on the official tape."

"Keep watching." Justin waited for the incriminating moment.

His dad's jaw dropped. He stopped the tape, rewound it, and played part of it over again. "If this is the real deal, how did we miss that?"

"I'm beginning to suspect it was the same way I walked out of Gordon's apartment with this video, unseen."

Mark stopped the tape and just stood there, running his hands through his hair.

"But that means there's someone out there with your abilities."

"And used them to make you see what they wanted you to see." Justin said.

"It also means that Dawn had outside help, but who?"

"Only three people have watched this: you're one, another is dead," Justin reminded him.

"Dr. Siffer?"

"When Gordon was alone to watch this and saw what we just saw, he probably reported it to Siffer. He's dead now. You don't have the Nephilim gene. He's the only choice left."

"If he covered this up, it means he's probably behind the actual theft as well. You said you found active nanobots in Gordon's body?"

"Siffer is covering up something. Why kill Gordon, unless he had other plans for the nanobots and Gordon got in the way?"

"This is a lot to take in all at once," Mark said. "I need time to think. Unfortunately son, it looks like Dawn is involved too."

"It might explain her behavior tonight. I think her conscience was beginning to bother her."

"Let's keep this quiet for now. If Siffer is dangerous, I don't want you getting in his way."

Justin hesitated. "Uh, it's way too late for that."

"What do you mean?"

"The vision returned tonight but it was much clearer. I saw the man who tried to abort me. It was Dr. Siffer."

Chapter 16

Beverly, while not openly admitting it, even to herself, had actually looked forward to Justin's visits lately. He was good at what he did and she decided to let him know how pleased she was with his work. She'd gotten to know him and felt safe enough that complimenting him wouldn't go to his head. For a kid with special abilities, he was very unassuming. He was a simple, down-to-earth teenager and was much easier to get along with than many guys her own age.

Lately, her issues with guys had preoccupied her thoughts. She'd heard the nicknames whispered around the office, including 'Hardball Heartstone' and 'Heart-O-Stone'. No one dared to call her that to her face, although she secretly wore the name proudly. Used to, anyway. Second thoughts about the tough-as-nails image were growing more frequent. After all, she had a soft, gentle side too.

A growing, mutual respect had developed in this working relationship with Justin. At times he could be frustrating, but she found herself trusting him enough to let her guard down when they were together.

Whatever it was that Justin contributed to the dynamics of this team, it made her feel good. It was refreshing. She insisted on one condition, however, and he had agreed to it. He was never to use his soul-searching powers on her. Anything he wanted to learn about her must be through old-fashioned way conversation.

He was late for their meeting. What could be keeping him?

****

Justin's level of frustration with Derrick hit an all time high. "You're not serious!" he exploded. "You were right, he is evil."

"That's great. Just turn against the guy who got you that newspaper job," Derrick argued.

"When this news gets out, he's going to prison."

Derrick suddenly staggered forward, pressing his hands against his temples. He looked pale, his skin clammy. Justin tried to steady him, but got pushed away.

"Get off me," he spat, "He's the best thing that could happen to this state."

****

Justin ran up the stairs, skipping every other one, and arrived at Beverly's office out of breath.

Her door was open, so he knocked on the doorjamb and walked in.

"Glad you could finally make it," she said.

"Sorry. Something big came up," he explained.

"Bigger than finding Senator Williams dead last night?"

"Williams? For real?"

"He just passed out and died," Beverly informed him.

Then Justin remembered the pictures took at the banquet. "I sensed something was up. He looked terrible. See?"

Beverly looked over the pictures. Another excellent set. Yes, the senator looked odd, distracted and maybe ill. He looked paler than usual. Justin had some not-too-complimentary close-ups.

"He was found dead in his room, an hour after his appearance at the banquet. Cerebral hemorrhage according to the coroner's office," Beverly added. "He would have…"

Justin stopped her short. "I've got more news for you."

"I had a feeling you would." Beverly said. "News follows you. What've you got?"

"Dr. Siffer is behind Gordon's death."

The look on Beverly's face said it all. "Where did you ever come up with that?"

Justin spent the next twenty minutes explaining the videotape, and what he believed was Siffer's role in the cover up. The irony of it all was the person who had complained the loudest about the stolen nanobots was the mastermind behind their theft.

"That's incredible. You think he's a Nephilim, like you?"

"Has to be. Gordon got to see a copy of the security tape without Siffer present to pull his mind tricks. He probably reported to Siffer what he wasn't supposed to have seen. It got him killed."

Following Justin's line of thinking, Beverly said, "The good doctor used the stolen nanobots to kill Gordon."

"Siffer has the scientific know-how and funds to reproduce nanobots. He needed the sample from the lab for a model. Once reprogrammed, they attacked Gordon's brain and he jumped to his death."

Beverly looked like she was letting this information sink in. "If I hadn't seen it with my own eyes, I'd have sent you packing long ago. Unfortunately, everything now makes sense—and it's scary. A murderous Nephilim is loose in Angel Falls."

"Siffer tried to prevent me from coming into the world eighteen years ago. Mr. Hardy, from my church, thinks Angel Falls is in some kind of peril. He may be right and I'm beginning to think Siffer's at the center of it. If what Mr. Hardy says is true, I'm supposed to stop him somehow."

"I'm sorry about Dawn, Justin. I know you cared about her," Beverly said.

"It's difficult to figure people out sometimes," Justin said. "Even with my so-called 'gift'."

Beverly reached across her desk and put her hand on Justin's forearm. "It's not your fault, Justin. You're a caring guy and you can't control everyone else's behavior."

"Derrick turned on me today, too. That's why I was late. Suddenly he thinks Siffer's the greatest. I tried to warn him, but he wanted to punch me."

Beverly squeezed his arm and stood to look out of her office window. Traffic and pedestrians moved freely about in the streets below, completely unaware of the danger descending on Angel Falls. "You guys will work it out," she said. "Lately, the reports crossing my desk make me wonder whether all of Angel Falls hasn't been infected with nanobots!"

No sooner had the words left her mouth... She swung around to face Justin. "Williams!"

Justin understood. "You think nanobots killed the senator?"

"How does one man, with strong convictions like Wilson had, suddenly decide to vote for someone he's categorically denounced in the past? I saw him on TV two days ago; he acted like a possessed robot. Now he's dead. In his last couple of TV appearances, he looked like something was eating him. Gordon was just the first.

Justin agreed. "You have some influence with the coroner's office. We need to get Wilson's blood under the microscope. Now that this has escalated, and my dad knows what's going on, he can get us into the 'scope at GenEx Labs."

Beverly said she would call the coroner and Dr. Thyme to set something up. If they found nanobots in the senator's body, it would strengthen their case against Dr. Siffer, especially if Justin was right about how he covered up the security video.

Beverly looked at Justin. "You've read the news," she began cautiously. "I don't think Gordon and Wilson are his only victims."

"What do you mean?"

"Think about it. Citizens are fighting in the streets over Siffer. Unexpected, dramatic increases in polling data in Siffer's favor. Suddenly, his political opponents rally to his support. They're committing political suicide, literally. It's statewide, not just here in Angel Falls. Siffer now has the wherewithal to reproduce these nanobots in large quantities. He's using them to poison the voters—probably your friend Derrick, too!"

"Until this morning, he hated Siffer, called him a crook," Justin said. "He looked sick too, unsteady on his feet."

"Derrick was at the banquet last night?"

"Yeah, why?"

"Siffer's been holding these banquets all over the state. Let me see those pictures."

Justin handed her his shots from the banquet. She rifled through them until she found what she wanted.

"I thought this looked familiar," Beverly said, holding up a picture of the enormous fountain of punch. "This thing has been the centerpiece at all his banquets. I'd bet top dollar this is how he gets the public to ingest those things. In fact, I'm sure of it. And look at this data. Wherever one of Siffer's banquets is held, street violence erupts just days later—without exception."

She showed him the picture of Derrick taking a drink of the nanobot-laced punch. The image hit Justin hard.

"I'm beginning to see that your presence here is no accident, Justin. We need to fight fire with fire, one Nephilim against another." Beverly said. "Siffer failed to stop you once for a reason. I think, with God's help and the Tribune behind us, we can take him down."

"Do you pray?" Justin asked her.

"Not until today, Justin. But I'm beginning to appreciate your friend's faith. I'm just starting to see a lot of things."

"Me too," Justin confessed. "And right now, Derrick needs my help."

Beverly fell back into her chair and looked directly into his eyes. "Justin, all of Angel Falls needs your help."

Chapter 17

It was like everyone and his brother decided to drive the Interstate at that moment. And nobody was in a hurry. Justin weaved his 98 Civic around the slower cars while CPU looked for the Ashland exit.

"I don't know whether to scream at these slowpokes or be thankful," Justin said.

CPU folded the map to a more manageable size and stared out the window. "Getting a case of nerves, huh?"

"What do I say to her? What if seeing me upsets her?"

"There's only one way to find out: get there and see what happens. You can't control everything you know."

Justin longed for simpler days, when he knew what people expected of him. Go to class, get average grades, do homework, and spend time with his friends. Fortunately, CPU had avoided Siffer's nanobot cocktail.

"Derrick's not talking to me," Justin said.

"He's not himself."

Justin managed a smile. "I'm glad your brain was spared. I hate finding my way on the Interstate alone!"

"Siffer's nanobots have killed two people so far. What about the others who drank the punch?" CPU asked.

"I know. Siffer must have made a special batch for everyone else. There'd be no one left alive to vote for him if he didn't."

"You hope."

"Siffer's powers must be limited if he needed the nanobots to pull this off."

"You're his biggest threat, but I wouldn't underestimate him just yet." CPU thought a moment and then asked, "Why do you suppose he hasn't come after you directly, yet?"

"Too risky. He's got an image to maintain, especially now that he's in the middle an election. But I think he has tried, indirectly."

"The parking lot incident?"

"That could be one."

CPU asked, "There were others?"

"That crazy wind storm that almost blew me off the plateau. It was like the forces of nature came to life and had it in for me."

"You sound a little nutty. You don't actually think Siffer can control the weather, do you?"

"No. But you had to have been there. It was eerie, like it was personal."

CPU alternated his gaze between the map, the window, and back to the map. "The exit should be coming up soon."

Justin breathed a deep sigh and thought about the nurse who saved his life. Hazel Wood must be about eighty-seven. Justin hoped she would be able to confirm his interpretation of the vision, her mental state permitting. He had no idea what eighty-seven years had done to her. It had to be Siffer in the vision. If it was, he guessed Siffer had probably been planning to take control of everything for a very long time.

That Hazel had defeated him, and survived, was impressive. If Dawn was involved, Siffer must have something on her. Unless - the idea sickened him - she was working for him voluntarily.

"Here's the turn," CPU said. "The home is just a mile from here, on the left."

****

Ashland Manor spread out over seventy-five acres, below rolling grassland hills. Justin assumed that its bright, pleasant exterior masked a gloomy interior. He remembered how visits to his grandmother were awfully depressing. They left a lasting, unpleasant impression on him. She'd become a shadow of the vibrant woman she once was, in a place just like this.

What he found inside was totally unexpected. In the center of a whirlwind of cheerful activity was an elderly woman, glowing with an energy that reflected off the smiles on everyone else's face.

Hazel moved among the residents, offering cheer and goodwill. Her laughter echoed from one end of a room to the other. Here was hope, a will to thrive; this was not a place for the solemn or anyone with a death wish.

Here was Hazel. This had to be the woman who had saved his life: Justin could feel it.

The receptionist called Hazel over to meet them and found them a quiet place to talk. Her demeanor instantly put the boys at ease. She thanked them for the unexpected, yet welcome, visit.

"You remind me of my grandson," Hazel told CPU. "He knows all about computers, too. Gave me one for Christmas—I just love it. Technology is wonderful and email is marvelous!"

Hazel gave CPU a quick pat on the head and turned toward Justin. She was about to say something, but stopped abruptly and stared deeply into his eyes. It felt like being a specimen under a microscope. Suddenly, her facial expression changed from being perplexed to one of wonder.

"Where are you boys from?"

Justin fidgeted, cleared his throat, and told her. "Angel Falls."

"You're eighteen?"

"Yes."

"That scar on your chin..." Tears suddenly welled up in her eyes. She reached her arms out to cradle Justin's face in her hands. "You must be the child." She patted the side of his face and stroked his hair.

Embarrassed, Justin looked down at the floor.

Hazel sat back, wiped her eyes, and told them her story. She explained how she had found faith in the Lord late in life while employed at an abortion clinic in Angel Falls. Her life had become a mass of conflicting emotions. She tried to justify her position there with the work performed by the clinic.

One day she realized she couldn't stay there any longer. Lives were being torn apart as women tried to manage the guilt and depression they felt over what they had done.

Then she heard the testimony of a young woman who had survived an abortion. God had ordained the days of her life, had 'knit her in her mother's womb'. Her life had value and she held no bitterness towards those who had tried to end it prematurely.

"I knew then that I wanted to serve this woman's God," she said. "Are you boys Christians?"

"Absolutely," CPU said. "We did a lot of praying before we got here."

"I wasn't sure how you'd react, when you found out who I was," Justin confessed.

"Nonsense." Hazel clapped her hands together. "This is an answer to my prayers."

"Tell us about Doctor Siffer," CPU blurted.

Hazel's body stiffened instantly. Wringing her hands together she said, "He's an awful man."

Justin became apologetic. "Sorry Mrs. Wood, but I know about the attempt on my life and how you saved me. Was Dr. Siffer the person carrying out the abortion?"

"After declaring my faith in God, I was immediately put to the test," Hazel began. "I was scheduled to assist with an abortion the very next night. That man had the poor woman so frightened. The abortion seemed to be more his idea than hers."

"So, it was Siffer?" Justin asked.

"Yes. I was terrified of him. He filled a room with the stench of death. Why he was in such a hurry he didn't even bother to remove his hat and cape during the procedure!"

Justin nodded knowingly at CPU.

Hazel continued. "I felt so weak, ashamed. He's a difficult man to stand up to. I helped him, even though I vowed that no more children would die at my hands."

"But you came back," Justin said.

"Siffer is an awful, frightening man. But, Isaiah says, 'The Lord Almighty is the one you are to fear, He is the one you are to dread and He will

152

be a sanctuary'. I went back to find you just in time."

Justin now had the confirmation he had sought. Suddenly he was more certain than ever that he was chosen to stop Siffer.

They sat and talked with Hazel about subjects that are more pleasant for a while longer. Without divulging his secret, Justin caught Hazel up on his life these past eighteen years. He thanked her again for being there for him and mentioned that he was currently enjoying his job as a Tribune photographer.

"Now that I'm on to him, I won't be taking any more photos of the campaign," Justin said. "But I've been wondering why he got me the job in the first place?"

Hazel smiled. Reaching for Justin's hands, she said, "That Siffer is a sly one. I used to hear him say, 'Keep your friends close, your enemies closer'."

"He was just keeping an eye on me."

"Remember, 'The righteousness of the blameless will direct his way aright, but the wicked will fall by his own wickedness'."

Justin recognized the quote from Proverbs, but didn't feel too confident that he could stay out of Siffer's way. They seemed destined to be on a collision course.

Hazel told Justin how she fought her battles through prayer and she spent several hours a day interceding on behalf of others. Justin had been praying more lately too. It encouraged him to know this prayer warrior was on his side. Now she was armed with more specific prayer requests. But he withheld his theory regarding Siffer's Nephilim nature from Hazel, to avoid upsetting her.

He changed the subject and asked about his mother. It was getting late and Hazel looked tired. But she seemed eager to describe things she'd kept bottled up all these years.

Apparently, Siffer hadn't anticipated any complications, but when Justin's mother began to bleed internally, he rushed out of the clinic, carrying the woman in his arms. Hazel assumed he was taking her to the nearest emergency room.

"Siffer got me to lock up when he left. I started home, but the image of you in a trashcan was unbearable. I went right back, wrapped you up, and brought you to GenEx Labs."

"What happened to my mother? Don't the hospitals have a record of her being treated that night?"

"I never saw your mother after that night, Justin. I was so concerned for your survival..."

"Did you look into her whereabouts?"

"I quit the clinic and packed my things. There was no way I wanted to run into that man, not after what I'd done. But before I put Angel Falls behind me for good, I checked the local hospitals.

No one matching your mother's description or condition had been admitted recently."

"Siffer, tying up another 'loose end', " CPU said.

"Three weeks later, after I settled into my new location, I read about her death in the paper," Hazel said.

"Did Siffer do it?" Justin asked her.

"He's too clever to ever get close to trouble. But I have no doubt in my mind."

"Don't you miss Angel Falls?" CPU asked.

"I have no family, had no friends—the few I had from the clinic didn't see eye-to-eye with me anymore. I found a good church here in Ashland and made plenty of new friends."

"How did you avoid Siffer?" Justin wanted to know.

"With no roots or family ties, I was able to leave town quickly. Siffer went on an overseas business trip. I never saw him again. To this day, I know it was the hand of God protecting me."

After a few more minutes of reminiscing, the boys got up to leave. Hazel led them down the hall toward the main entrance. On the way out, Justin turned to Hazel. "I have no idea what I'm supposed to do next."

"Trust God to work," she said. "Our understanding is limited. God always works, sometimes in spite of our efforts."

Chapter 18

The last time Beverly did some hands-on investigative work was two years ago, as an intern with another paper. On the surface, Senator Williams' death looked like a cerebral hemorrhage, aggravated by the stress of his job. He had been in poor health lately, as well. Beverly knew differently, but there would be no autopsy unless the death was ruled as suspicious. So, she called in a favor at the police station and had them open up an investigation. This led to an autopsy and, sure enough, she was right about the nanobots.

Tom Selden, the lead detective in the Gordon case, was four years Beverly's senior. The two were good friends and even dated once or twice, but ultimately, both were married to their jobs. She watched him shuffle papers on his desk in an effort to straighten up a bit before they talked. The atmosphere of the station was a lot like Tom's desk - chaotic. Beverly couldn't think of when she saw this many officers at the station at one time.

A chair flew through the air almost striking one officer. Three other officers tackled and cuffed the detainee responsible.

Tom got up to shut the door to his office. This proved to be only slightly effective in shutting out the noise. "What you're doing could get dangerous, Bev."

"Look outside your office, Tom. It already is."

A fistfight had erupted between two other men being held, as several more officers intervened.

"Considering what's at stake," Tom said, "We handled everything very inconspicuously. I saw those robot things Morris had in his head myself. Bev, if you're found out, you could end up on a slab next to him."

She leaned in and smiled in mock flirtation. "I can be inconspicuous too, Tom. And I'll have you to watch my back."

"Flattery won't help. The department is overworked as it is. Look out there, we're stretched to the limit. Leave the investigating to the pros."

"Hey, I am a pro. Besides, I have additional resources."

"You mean that kid you mentioned? If I didn't know you better, I'd think you were getting sweet on him."

"Don't be silly, he's too young."

"Then, what's he got that I don't? You two sure spend a lot of time together," he teased.

Beverly's face turned red and she got angry. "He's bright and very resourceful, with connections to GenEx and Siffer's campaign headquarters. Don't make more of it than it is."

Tom laughed. "Methinks you protest too much."

Beverly ignored him.

He picked up the report on Senator Williams' autopsy and tossed it across his desk. "At first, I thought you were nuts. What tipped you off?"

"Let's just say it was a hunch, based on some other information I picked up recently."

Having moved beyond Tom's skepticism, she was ready to do her own searching.

A powerful man like Siffer would not be easy to take down. She needed proof to tie him directly to the nanobots. If it were up to the police, the trail of evidence would turn ice cold before they finished gingerly tiptoeing around the gubernatorial candidate. They had protocols to adhere to; she did not. She wouldn't be swayed by public opinion, either, even if it was nanobot-induced.

"Just be careful. Siffer's billions make him very resourceful and dangerous," Tom reminded her.

When their meeting ended, Tom walked her downstairs to the exit, keeping an eye out for more flying chairs. They hugged, and Beverly turned to leave, but stopped suddenly.

"One last question, Tom. Who paid the Stoltzfus girl's bail?"

"Siffer. Why?"

Beverly smiled. "There's my connection."

****

The drive home from Ashland was more relaxing.

"Glad you went?" CPU asked.

"Hazel's amazing," Justin said. "She keeps that whole place hopping."

"That kind of power has to be greater than anything Siffer has," CPU said confidently.

"She's very modern, too. I couldn't believe she set up her own wireless Internet connection. I can't even do that."

Suddenly, a high-pitched noise assaulted Justin's ears. He lost his grip on the steering wheel. It slipped from his hands and his car swerved sharply into oncoming traffic. The noise came from CPU, who was screeching like a banshee.

"CPU, what on earth is the matter?" Justin yelled. It was not without a bit of anger at being startled and almost killed.

CPU was jumping in his seat, stretching the seatbelt to its limit. He said it again, only not nearly as loud as a moment ago, "I've got it."

A truck missed them by inches as Justin struggled to steer back into his lane.

"I know how to neutralize the nanobots."

"Can't you have quieter brainstorms? You almost got us killed."

CPU tried to calm himself. "Sorry."

His plan involved getting into GenEx Labs after hours. If Justin used his powers to get them past the guards, he could study the software used to control the nanobots. He said that if he could make sense of the software, he could reverse the curse Siffer had brought upon Angel Falls - and Derrick. But he wouldn't spill the rest of the plan until he studied the software. However, deep inside he was sure he could do it.

Justin smiled widely. "If anyone can pull this off, you're the one."

****

Beverly, disguised, took a seat behind one of many desks equipped with a phone. She moved slowly, deliberately. Her disguise consisted of a long auburn wig, dark sunglasses, and a white cane. It seemed to be working. The staffer who provided her with half an hour of telephone training appeared to be convinced that she was a blind woman named Stefanie.

As inconspicuously as possible, 'Stefanie' placed her over-sized handbag near the right edge of the desk and looked around Siffer's campaign headquarters. Inside the bag, thanks to one of her FBI friends, was a high-powered listening device.

She aimed the bag toward the office she had had learned earlier was Siffer's and prepared to listen in on his conversations. The small receiver, placed inside her ear, looked like a hearing aid. It was barely visible. She moved the phone further to the left to avoid blowing out her eardrum if it rang. Struck with a genius idea, she pulled the phone cord out of the back of the phone. She hoped not to be around long enough for anyone to notice.

It was the perfect disguise for the circumstances, since she needed the sunglasses were necessary to avoid Siffer's Nephilim stare. The game would be up if Siffer got suspicious and penetrated her mind. Yet, wearing sunglasses indoors might draw unwanted attention. That's when she came up with the blind angle. A white cane would answer anyone's questions about wearing sunglasses indoors.

Beverly reached inside her bag to switch on the device and her ear suddenly filled with noise. She could make out two voices—a man's and a woman's. One was clearly Siffer's, obviously in a bad mood.

"I raised you like you were my own, because your mother couldn't and this is how you repay me?" Siffer's voice crackled in her ear.

"She couldn't live with what you were," The woman appeared to reply through tears. Static in the earpiece made it difficult to tell.

"Keep it down. You're overwrought and talking nonsense."

In a hushed, angry tone, the woman growled, "I won't end up like her."

"Fine. I'll take care of this myself. You, on the other hand, can pack your things. I'm sending you back."

Beverly saw Siffer's office door swing open violently, hitting the wall behind it. A young woman stormed out. The woman looked up, appearing to be somewhat embarrassed by her display. Beverly immediately recognized Dawn, who rushed past her desk and out through the main exit. Not wanting to lose sight of her, Beverly grabbed her bag and followed her out.

****

Siffer emerged from his office, just in time to see a blind woman sprint toward the exit. Curiously, she weaved her way past multiple obstacles with ease, apparently in pursuit of Dawn. He walked over to the recently vacated desk and looked around.

The phone was unplugged.

He looked over at a volunteer in the next desk and asked, "Who was sitting here, just a minute ago?""

An older man, just finishing a call, looked up, paused a moment, then said, "Someone new, just started this afternoon in fact."

Siffer felt his patience draining away. "Did she have a name?"

"I thought I heard someone call her Stefanie. Sorry, that's all. I never spoke with her."

Siffer plugged the phone cord back in and found one of the staffers in charge of new recruits.

"She's gone already? She was here less time than it took to train her," the staffer said.

"Do you remember her name - it was Stefanie something?"

"Goodman. Stefanie Goodman, the blind woman. She really left?"

"Yes. Do you remember anything else about her?"

"She didn't say much. Just wanted to know which office was yours. She specifically requested that empty desk over there."

"Didn't anything about that behavior strike you as odd?"

"Not really. I figured she wanted to be close to the rest rooms."

Siffer snorted something and told the staffer to forget their conversation. He then ordered him to go back to whatever he was doing. A frown of concentration formed on Siffer's face. There was something familiar about that name. He looked down at the once-disconnected phone cord, snorted again, and rushed back to his office and locked the door.

****

Beverly followed Dawn on foot for three blocks until, after several quick, sideward glances,

Dawn got into her car and headed west. Fortunately, Beverly's car was not far from the same spot. She deliberately parked several blocks away so no one at Siffer's headquarters would witness a blind woman parallel park.

Dawn's red Cabriolet was easy to spot from a safe following distance. In fact, it was almost too easy. She made no sudden turns. She even slowed to below the speed limit once in a while.

After fifteen minutes, they were heading up a gravel road on the southern side of the plateau outside town. Beverly slowed her car to keep her distance, but figured Dawn had to know she was being followed by now. There was no one else around for miles.

Was she meeting someone at the lake? It suddenly occurred to her that Dawn could have lured her here.

She rounded a corner, past heavy underbrush, and stopped short. Dawn's car sat, unoccupied, about thirty feet away. Beverly yanked back on the parking brake, ripped off her wig and sunglasses, and got out to look for Dawn on foot. She followed the narrow, timeworn path through heavy thickets to a clearing across from the lake. Dawn was standing on the other side of the clearing, very close to the waterfall's edge.

Beverly called out to her as she approached, but Dawn didn't respond. Her gaze was fixed on the churning water hundreds of feet below. The updraft kept blowing her hair into her face, which she did not attempt to brush aside.

"Dawn?" Beverly called again, over the roar of the falls.

Dawn turned, surprised. "Who are you? What do you want?" she demanded.

"You're in some serious trouble. What's Siffer got on you?" Beverly asked.

"What's it matter any more?" Dawn shouted. She looked away.

"We know you're a thief. Siffer's using the nanobots to control people and some are dying because of it. Is he controlling you too?"

"I'm done with him." Dawn moved a step closer to the edge.

"Then help us stop him. Come back to town with me." Beverly took a few cautious steps towards her.

"You don't understand..."

Beverly moved in closer. Dawn's reddened eyes stared vacantly and it was obvious she had been crying.

"You can't stop him." Dawn said.

"Justin and I disagree."

Dawn seemed to come to life for a moment at the mention of Justin. "He's all right?"

"Does that mean you care? You have an odd way of showing it."

Dawn's blank expression returned, as she took another step toward the edge. "He'll turn...they all do..."

"What are you talking about? Help us..." Beverly moved in, reaching out to Dawn, but stopped in horror. Dawn took one final step, her foot landing on air. She fell, silently, disappearing into the thunderous, churning waters below.

Beverly frantically groped about in her pockets for her cell phone when she remembered it was back in her car. Scrambling back through the path, thorns scratching her face and arms, she reached her car and yanked at the door handle.

It was locked. Force of habit from years of city living. Her keys were still dangling in the ignition. She hurried around back and tested the trunk. It opened. She climbed in, kicked the rear seat down, and crawled inside. Grabbing the phone from between the front seat cushions, she frantically dialed 911. The voice at the other end instructed her to wait at the scene until an officer arrived.

Beverly closed the phone, fell back into the rear seat of her car, and exhaled heavily. The image of Dawn, dropping like a rag doll, burned in her brain. Only then did she notice that her hands were trembling.

And Dawn's car was gone.

Chapter 19

Tom disliked interrogating Beverly like this and she could tell. The way he paced around his desk, chin in his hand, thinking out loud. He was upset.

"They'll say you lured her up there..." he began.

Beverly jumped in, "Tom, I followed her."

"I know, but there are no witnesses to any of this - her car wasn't even there! One of my men found it in a parking garage at the other end of town."

"That's impossible. It was there, she drove it and no one else was there with us."

"As far as you know," Tom said.

"Can't you check for tread marks?"

"We're working the entire area, Bev."

Beverly groaned with exasperation. "What purpose would I have to get rid of her?"

"Jealousy?" Tom gave her a sideways glance and prepared for the outburst.

"Come on. You know that's absurd."

"I might know that, but if this suicide turns out to be a murder case, you're our prime suspect. Would a jury find it absurd? Are you sure you don't have even the slightest feelings for that kid?"

Beverly sat back, arms folded across her chest. "No more than I have for you," she said with a sneer.

"Ouch. Look, if you showed even the slightest feelings for Justin to a jury, you'd hang yourself. I'm just trying to help."

"Are you arresting me?"

"I'm just letting you know what direction this could take. No one's being arrested yet; we're still collecting evidence."

"Her body hasn't been found, has it?" Beverly asked. "You won't have a case if a body isn't produced!"

"She was probably dashed to pieces by the rocks below and washed down river, piece by piece. It's a strong current, we might never recover her remains."

It was a comforting and repulsive idea at the same time. All Beverly had wanted to do was talk to the girl. She held no animosity for Dawn, who was clearly a troubled human being.

She felt her own anger well up as she remembered the way Dawn had strung Justin along. The strong feelings caught her by surprise. She flinched.

Tom noticed and he asked, "What's wrong?"

She quickly found control, "The realization of a trial, it upset me."

Tom was right. She'd have to manage her feelings more closely over the next several weeks.

"Well, don't worry. Staying at the scene and calling it in was the best thing you could've done."

"You haven't said, 'I told you so', yet," Beverly said.

"You're too personally involved in this. That's one reason why I told you to leave the police work to us. If you insist on running your own investigation, I can't protect you."

"I'll keep a low profile, I promise," Beverly said. "But keep me informed. You know I can't just sit on this and do nothing."

"Don't you have a job to do?" Tom indicated the door. "Get out of here. Go to work or something."

Beverly started for the door and stopped. "Dawn may have been related to Dr. Siffer, maybe his niece."

"You know this, how?" Tom asked.

"I overheard them arguing. One thing's for sure, Siffer raised Dawn and knew her mother – and apparently her mother did not fare so well in her relationship with the doctor."

****

Work sounded like good therapy right now. She left Tom's office and realized there'd be several late evenings of catching up ahead of her. And, after hours, she would have the full resources of the Tribune to continue her own investigation.

An hour and a half later, after a shower and a late lunch, Beverly was back at her office. The familiarity of her desk felt good. She finally regained a level of composure that enabled her to concentrate on the news of Angel Falls.

Unfortunately, her objectivity concerning Siffer was gone. So, she decided to concentrate on GenEx news and pass the election coverage on to one of her subordinates. By working on the GenEx case, she could disclose enough details to expose Siffer for the kind of threat he actually was. All bets would be off as far as the election was concerned. If only she could find more concrete evidence.

****

The Thymes' doorbell rang. Justin looked out to see CPU on the other side, school bag in one hand and a laptop under his arm. As always, he was wearing that same grin.

Justin let him in. "Hurry up, let's get this over with."

"How much time do I have?" CPU asked.

"Two hours. Is that enough?"

"Sure. Where's your dad's laptop?"

Justin led him to a coffee table where the laptop sat, waiting for the login password. A radio quietly played oldies nearby.

"I can't get in," Justin said, pointing at the cursor in the password field.

CPU opened the laptop's CD-ROM drawer, pulled a CD from his school bag, placed it in the drive, and rebooted.

"Once I reset his password, we'll be in," he said.

CPU reset the password and logged in after another reboot. On the desktop was a shortcut to something called 'Bot-Prot'. CPU ran it. He took some time to study what it could do. One of the menu items brought up a second screen, with the outline of a human form in the center.

"Something's missing," CPU said.

Justin thought a moment. "The transceiver."

CPU nodded. "It picks up signals from the bots and displays their location in the human subject."

"Do you need it to reprogram the bots?"

"Not necessarily. To detect the nanobots you need it, but they can receive programming through any uplink, as long as it's on the correct frequency. This software adjusts that."

"You said not necessarily. What's the catch?"

"I'd need the transceiver to make the initial contact, and then determine their frequency. Once I have that, any device could return the signal using this software. Just set the software to the right sending frequency."

CPU pulled his cell phone from the school bag. "That's where this comes in. Once I lock on to their frequency, my cell phone becomes a modem. I dial out, using the frequency set on the software, only this time with new programming instructions. Every repeater tower in Angel Falls, even the whole state, will stop those bots dead."

CPU sat back, looking very pleased with himself.

"There's just one problem," Justin said. "The only transceiver is at the lab. My dad would miss his laptop if we took it with us."

"I can copy the entire program to my laptop. It's not very secure software - I'm surprised. It doesn't even use an install routine."

"Probably because it's mostly useless outside the lab," Justin said. "We'll need to break into the lab. The delivery elevator is the only security weakness I know."

"How'd they overlook that?"

"They didn't. They would just never expect a Nephilim to pass through one."

CPU pulled a USB flash drive from his bag and plugged it into the laptop. When he finished copying the software directory, he transferred it to his laptop. Then, he created a desktop shortcut to the program's executable file and performed a test run.

"There it is, see?"

"Like magic," Justin said.

"Your magic is what we'll need to get inside."

Justin shut down the laptop, returned it to its case and its usual spot beside his dad's recliner. Tonight would be their best opportunity to get inside GenEx. Summertime meant a lighter workforce at the labs. Better yet, there'd be no moon out tonight.

"We need to do this quickly before anyone else becomes a victim of this stuff," Justin said.

CPU suddenly sounded distressed. "What if your nanobots are disabled by this?"

"It's a chance we'll have to take. Derrick is in worse shape than I'd be if my bots were turned off. We need to move fast."

"Where's Dawn been? Have you spoken with her lately?"

The radio answered CPU's question before Justin could. The unobtrusive background music suddenly turned into a jarring special report.

Dawn was dead in an apparent suicide, with Tribune editor, Beverly Heartstone, the only witness.

"He's gonna pay." Justin slammed his fist against the heavy oak coffee table, but jumped back in shock when it cracked down the middle and collapsed to the floor.

"Oops." He slumped back into the couch. "Sorry."

CPU silently gathered his things and started to leave. At the door, he turned and said, "Tonight is payback."

****

Justin arrived at Beverly's office about three-thirty in the afternoon in a bad way. He needed to find out what Beverly knew about Dawn. He must have looked pathetic because, when Beverly saw him, she surprised him with a hug.

It was a little embarrassing at first.

"I'm so sorry, Justin," she said. "You OK?"

He gave in to her comfort and for a whole minute just rested in her arms.

"I'll be OK," he finally said. "Siffer did this to her, didn't he?"

"Those two have a history," she said, returning to her seat. Justin sat down across from her.

"What do you mean?"

"They go back a-ways. Siffer knew her mother. And she was working for him."

"And using me, wasn't she?"

"I think she regretted it in the end."

"Why didn't she just come to us for help?"

"I don't know," Beverly said. "But if this is the way things turn out for anyone associated with that man, we're all in a lot of trouble if he's elected."

Chapter 20

A cloudy, moonless night should have been perfect for sneaking into GenEx, but when they arrived, Justin had second thoughts. The building loomed large and black in front of them; not even the generator-powered emergency lights were on. Something wasn't right. The place looked like an enormous crypt. A sudden chill ran up his spine.

With laptop in hand, CPU followed him to the express elevator across from the parking lot. These elevators did not connect directly to the main security system, like the public access elevators. It wasn't necessary because each elevator required activation by a unique key. Every driver underwent a strict screening process before acquiring one of these keys. Those keys were the extent of security at the delivery elevators, but they proved to be very effective. Besides, all of the drivers were actually trained GenEx employees who valued their jobs enough to stay honest.

If Justin could get them in this elevator, they could exit the same way without setting off the alarms.

"Wait right here," he instructed CPU, "until I pass through these doors. When I open them from the inside, we'll be good to go."

Justin pressed against the elevator, closed his eyes, and in an instant was gone. He'd been practicing this move at home when no one was around. When the elevator opened up, he noticed how CPU's face registered disbelief.

CPU smiled. "I still can't get used to that."

"Don't stand there gawking, get in."

The elevator creaked and moaned, louder than usual in the dark, still night. It crept upward, inch by inch, echoing through the empty building until it finally reached the third floor. With an abrupt screech and a thump, it stopped. The doors slid open unceremoniously into a dark hallway. Oddly, no security personnel were in sight. The only footsteps they heard were their own as they cautiously felt their way along the hallway.

"I can't see a thing," CPU whispered.

"I can. My eyes can adjust. The lab's over here, to the left. The walls have handrails. Hold onto one and follow it to the next room."

CPU found the handrail. He listened for Justin's footsteps as he moved slowly to his left.

Suddenly, a low moan came from behind them. CPU grabbed Justin's shirt.

"Relax! It's just the elevator going back down."

They reached the swinging doors of the lab and slipped inside. Justin found a small desk lamp and turned it on. It emitted just enough light for CPU to do his thing without drawing attention to their work.

"That better?" Justin asked.

"Perfect. Just guard the door, please."

CPU located a small box on a table, next to a chair and a gurney, both with straps. "This must be the transceiver," he said. "They must tie their subject down on one of these and run the program from here."

"What do you think the range of that transceiver thing is?" Justin asked.

"From what I've read, maybe only a couple hundred feet, but once we're broadcasting over my phone's cellular network, it's virtually unlimited."

CPU flipped on the transceiver and fired up his laptop. A light on the transceiver blinked red, while CPU clicked on different functions in the software. Suddenly, his screen showed the same generic human form, this time covered with blue dots. The light on the transceiver now glowed with a steady green light.

"Look! These blue dots must represent you."

Justin came around to look.

"Hey, I'm locked out," CPU said. "All the standard programming buttons are disabled."

"So, I'm safe?"

"I don't know, maybe. There might be some degree of incompatibility with your old nanobots and this new software. I've learned that the color of the dots on this monitor will change base on a variety of factors."

"Like what?"

"Nanobots emit signatures based on their version of hardware technology, programming and software, and other factors. I fell asleep before I finished the article."

Another moan, almost a low growl, came from somewhere beyond the lab doors.

CPU looked anxiously at Justin. "The elevator, again?"

"Not this time..."

"Justin, look." The screen in front of him suddenly displayed a second human form.

With red dots.

Justin quickly reached for the desk lamp and turned it off. The moan echoed down the halls again, only louder and closer this time. The sound of shuffling feet became evident.

Both boys froze, looking toward the doors, their faces eerily reflecting the light from the laptop.

The shuffling stopped.

Justin looked over at CPU and whispered, "Is the software compatible with these red ones?"

"Picking up their signal, loud and clear."

"But, can you disable them?"

"Way ahead of you..." CPU's mouse moved madly across the screen, clicking all the appropriate buttons.

Another angry moan.

"CPU, how's it coming?"

"Could be better."

"What's that mean?"

The lab doors flew open. A pair of red, glowing beads pierced the dark lab. They scanned back and forth in unison.

CPU barely croaked out a screech, "What is that?"

Justin could make out the dark form of a man, his blank eyes burning bright red. As light from the laptop fell across the form, the boys recognized the GenEx security uniform. The guard raised his nightstick and let out a vicious howl.

Justin waved his arms in an attempt to keep his attention away from CPU. The nanobot-controlled creature started toward him.

"He's under Siffer's control. Shut him down."

"I'm trying!"

****

Showing ten-thirty, the clock on the wall told Beverly she had spent enough time at the Tribune. A lot more digging needed to be done, but this was enough progress for one day. She was tired. Without a doubt, Siffer would soon be exposed for what he was. She'd enjoy doing it too.

Beverly grabbed her bag and cell phone and headed towards the rear elevators. To avoid her usual conversation with Ray, the night watchman, Beverly parked in a side alley. She was in no mood to continue an on-going discussion of her dating habits with him tonight.

Except for one janitor cleaning the office next to the elevators, the floor was deserted. She fumbled through her bag for car keys while she waited for the elevator. Calm always settled through the building at this late hour. Beverly embraced it. She would soak the unpleasantness of the day away in a warm tub, enjoy some ice cream, a movie, and then go to bed.

The elevator arrived and seamlessly transported her to the first floor at the side of the building. Outside, one dim, solitary streetlamp reflected off her car, exaggerating the shadows that engulfed the rest of the alley. As her key slid into the lock, something rustled behind her.

"Hello?" Beverly stepped away from her car and looked back into the shadows. Nothing. She turned back toward her car and right into Siffer's face looming over her.

"Ms. Heartstone, a pleasure to run into you," Siffer said, his voice calm and cool. He spoke in evenly measured tones. "Working late?"

Her heart skipped a beat. Siffer was dressed to the nines, as usual, and wearing those stupid sunglasses. "Uh, Dr. Siffer, just the usual last-minute editing before tomorrow's edition hits the streets." Beverly tried to sound casual. By playing with her keys she hoped to hide the trembling in her hands.

"I have an errand for you," Siffer said. "You're going to kill Justin Thyme."

"Did you say, kill him?"

"And yourself, afterwards."

Beverly took a step backward. "The only thing I'm going to do for you is see that you're put away."

Siffer smiled confidently. "I had a feeling you'd react this way. No matter."

He reached under his cape and pulled out a small caliber pistol. Beverly gasped, taking another step backward. "What do you plan to do with that?"

"It's what you're going to do with it, Beverly," he said matter-of-factly. "You lured Dawn up to the falls and pushed her to her death. Now you will lure Justin to the same spot. You will shoot him with this." He danced the gun in front of her eyes.

"No one will believe—"

"That in a fit of jealousy you killed your rival and the young man she loved? Then, so despondent, you turned the gun on yourself. I assure you, once it's over, everyone will believe it."

He bared his teeth in a twisted smile, then slowly removed his sunglasses.

The sight of his eyes twisted Beverly's stomach into a terrified knot. They were red like blood. He looked right into hers. A tingly numbness flowed into her arms and legs.

"You see, Beverly, I know things about your heart, things you've hidden even from yourself. It will be easy for me to twist your feelings for that wretched boy into a jealous rage. It's the kind of story the world loves to read about."

Beverly felt her knees going weak as she steadied herself against her car. Siffer put the gun away, pulled out a syringe, and plunged it into Beverly's arm.

"This will probably hurt you more than it will hurt me," he said laughing.

Beverly fainted. Siffer caught her and carried her back into the shadows.

****

The possessed security guard growled again, swinging his nightstick wildly at Justin. The nightstick just missed his head by inches.

CPU frantically pounded away at the keyboard. He tried to override the laptop's programming with some of his own. "Why don't your mind tricks work on him?" CPU yelled. "How come he can see us?"

"I don't know. Nothing I do affects him." Justin jumped over a table to avoid another attack. "Why can't you stop him?"

"I'm almost there and I think I'm on to something."

Out of the corner of his eye, Justin caught CPU's fingers running, like an insane tap dancer, over the keyboard. At that instant, the guard's nightstick crashed hard against Justin's leg. It flew out of the guard's hand and shattered into wooden splinters.

"He can't hurt you," CPU said. "Keep him away for just a bit longer."

The guard howled in rage and lunged at Justin, only to receive an elbow in the chest that sent him sailing across the lab. He slammed into the far wall and dropped to the floor in a heap. A moment later, he jumped up screaming, fists clenched, flying toward Justin again.

Justin braced for the impact. "CPU, come on."

"This should do it." CPU punched the 'enter' key. "Now."

The guard pulled up short of Justin, clawing at his head with both hands. Suddenly the red glow in his eyes died and he fell to the floor.

"Is he...dead?" CPU asked.

Justin carefully felt his neck for a pulse. "No. But he'll probably be out cold for a long time."

"We have another problem," CPU said.

"Now what?"

"Siffer's a genius. I can access his nanobots through the program on this laptop, but I need to run multiple permutations of the program, in the correct sequence, in order to de-activate them."

Justin dragged the security guard to a more comfortable corner of the lab. "In English, please."

"I had to write another program to control the main one. That's what took so long. It would take days to figure out the sequence and execute it fast enough. With another program, the one I just wrote, it can be done in nanoseconds."

"So, what's your problem?" Justin asked.

CPU pointed over to the guard, lying peacefully in the corner. "The bots controlling the general population are different from Siffer's and yours. That means I need a test subject."

"Derrick," Justin said. "But we haven't been on the best of terms. How do I get him here?"

"You'll think of something," CPU said. "He's still susceptible to your mind tricks, unlike our friend over there on the floor. Once I'm sure I can deactivate Derrick's nanobots, the rest of Angel Falls will be easy."

Chapter 21

Beverly sat next to Siffer inside his black limousine. No one would ever see them, hidden deep within the shadows of the alley. Perspiration collected on her forehead. She couldn't think straight. A buzzing in her head brought searing pain each time she fought against Siffer's words. If she accepted Siffer's plan, however, the buzzing comforted her. Soon, she had no idea whether her thoughts were her own, or his.

"Your little disguise was quite charming, actually," Siffer said to her. "If you hadn't left that phone unplugged, I might never have become suspicious."

Siffer spoke with condescension and Beverly accepted it. She heard him, but was deaf to his words at the same time. It was as if she was watching herself carry on a one-way conversation with a total stranger from a mile away.

"I make it a point to know everything about everyone, my dear," he continued. "Goodman was your mother's maiden name. Stefanie is your middle name, which you never use. That's all it took." He smiled and stroked the hair away from her face. Beverly saw the sick smile and those red eyes, which continued to burn into her soul. It sickened her and the pain returned.

"You're coming around nicely," Siffer said as he handed her the gun. "I thought you'd be more troublesome, but that tough feminist exterior of yours is just a façade, isn't it?" He pointed to the now empty syringe, "These little darlings are already doing their work."

Siffer exited the limo. He walked around to the other side to open Beverly's door. Her feet were unsteady as he helped her out.

"You have your instructions, my dear. Now, get into your car, drive up to the falls, call that boy, and wait for him."

Beverly, from somewhere inside her head, watched as she shuffled to her car. She heard herself thinking, "If I can't have Justin, no one will."

****

Justin and CPU managed to come up with a pretense for getting Derrick to the lab. Derrick met Justin at the delivery elevator. Some of his offensive attitude had disappeared, giving Justin a little more confidence about what he had to do next. Still, his best friend was not himself and he appeared stressed, agitated, and pale. Justin knew it was the nanobots.

"CPU and I put together a TV ad to boost Siffer's campaign," Justin lied, hating to do it.

"I never thought you'd come around," Derrick said. "How did you get access to GenEx to make this?"

"My dad. He's a Siffer fan too. But we had to use the lab after hours." Last lie, he promised himself.

Justin led him up to the lab. He had him sit in what Derrick believed was a comfortable recliner. Justin prevented him from feeling the straps as he tightened them around his wrists and ankles. Then he nodded to CPU.

"Just watch the wall," he instructed. "It should last about fifteen minutes. Tell us what you think when it's over."

He walked over to CPU. "How long will it take you to deactivate him?" he asked.

"At least twenty minutes, less if I get lucky," CPU said and pushed his glasses back up his nose.

"And if it works? Then what?"

"I hook up my cell phone to the laptop, like a modem, and let the software dial out to every nanobot in the state. That should fix everyone."

Justin saw Derrick's image pop up on the software, covered with yellow dots. "They're different, like you thought they would be."

"You guys, I'm waiting. Where's the show?" Derrick said.

Justin quickly glanced over. "It takes a moment to set up but it's worth it."

A cell phone rang. Justin jumped.

"It's yours, not mine," CPU said.

Justin quickly reached for his phone. He flipped it open before it attracted any more unwanted attention. His face turned pale as he listened to the person on the other end.

"Now what?" CPU asked him.

"Beverly's at the falls. She needs me up there, right away."

Suddenly, another screen popped up on CPU's laptop.

"More red dots," CPU said anxiously. "Siffer's security force."

"You know how to handle them," Justin said. "You still have that program to stop them?"

"Sure. But what about him?" He nodded in Derrick's direction. "He's gonna take time."

Justin forced a smile. "You're the computer whiz, multitask."

"I don't like this."

"Beverly didn't sound right, real agitated. I have to go."

"I hope Derrick's restraints hold. If he catches on to what's really happening..."

"You'll be done before that happens. Besides, he's in restraints." Justin restored his cell phone to its belt clip and implanted an idea into Derrick's mind. Derrick leaned back and relaxed, looking very interested at whatever he thought he saw on the wall in front of him. Justin hoped the vision would last.

He gave CPU a last glance. Then, with a thumbs up, Justin cautiously slipped out of the lab.

Out in the hall, Justin stopped. He saw the guard still some way off, heading slowly toward the lab. He looked in the opposite direction, toward the elevator. He thought about CPU and started back to the lab when a mental picture of Beverly stopped him.

Derrick was tied down. CPU had already managed one security guard. Beverly was alone— she needed him. He tossed a mental coin and headed toward the elevator.

****

Summertime tourism made for heavier traffic, even at this late hour. The urgency in Beverly's voice made it difficult for Justin not to force slowpokes off the road. She had been skimpy with details, but had urged him to get to her quickly.

Fifteen minutes later, he was winding his way up the side of the plateau. He went as far as he could by car, parked, then ran the rest of the way through the heavy brush and trees.

The clearing came into view. The fall's distance from city lights made the evening even darker. He adjusted his eyes to see in the dark. The monument stood to his right. Beyond it, he could hear the mighty roar of Angel Falls.

But no Beverly.

He moved past the monument, cautiously eyeing the surrounding area for signs of another presence. He got as far as the falls without seeing a soul. Tons of water pounding against the rocks below had a mesmerizing affect. His eyes followed its course down river. Deep within its hypnotic presence, he caught himself thinking of Dawn.

Forcing his mind back into the present, dizziness suddenly overcame him. His fear of heights was taking over. Quickly, he took several steps back from the edge.

As he broke away from the river's view, he called, "Beverly." He turned with a start.

"Right behind you," Beverly said flatly.

"Are you all right?" Justin asked.

He took a step toward her and stopped when he saw a gun pointed right at him.

"Don't come any closer," she warned.

Chapter 22

CPU's fingers flew across the keyboard as sweat trickled down his temples. Derrick was restless. Was the vision wearing off, or was this a side effect of the nanobots?

"What's going on?" Derrick suddenly yelled. He yanked at his wrist and ankle restraints. "How did I get tied to this thing?"

The vision wore off.

"Hold on, Derrick, just a second," CPU said without missing a keystroke.

"I'll smash you. Get me out of this thing now."

"I'm undoing Siffer's damage - be quiet," CPU ordered. "You'll thank me later."

"What damage?"

"Your buddy filled you with mind-controlling nanobots. I'm trying to save you before they completely fry your brain."

Derrick pulled vigorously at the restraints. "You're crazy. Get me out of this."

Another red-dotted image popped up on the screen. CPU breathed a low warning, "Derrick, quiet. Someone's coming."

"Good." Derrick continued to pull frantically at the restraints, yelling at the top of his voice, "Help! Someone! Get me out of here!"

CPU moaned and switched gears. He minimized Derrick's program and brought up the red-dot one. He strained the old laptop to the limits of its processing power. The hourglass sat there for what seemed like an hour when the lab doors flew opened with a crash.

What Derrick saw turned him pale as a sheet. "What is that?" he screamed.

"More of your hero's handiwork." CPU typed quickly. The laptop responded sluggishly. "Come on," He urged the sluggish machine, hitting the keys harder. The guard howled in anger, smashing up the room as he lumbered toward CPU. His breathing was labored, his eyes burning red.

****

"Beverly, what's the matter?" Justin asked, taking another half step backwards.

"Dawn was all wrong for you," Beverly said, her eyes vacant. She stared right through him, her voice strained and distant. She struggled to get each word out.

"You look like you need a doctor," Justin said. He took one step towards her when a shot rang out.

He fell back and grabbed his left arm near the shoulder. He hit the ground hard as blood slowly seeped from where the bullet had grazed him.

Beverly lowered the gun, pointing it inches from Justin's face. His arm smarted, but he rolled, the next shot missing him by inches. He had to think fast. Accessing Beverly's mind, he made himself invisible.

Another shot rang out, the bullet flying into empty space. "Enough of your tricks," Beverly shouted. She swung around, the gun pointing in an arc, firing continuously as she turned. Several shots flew off aimlessly into the night. "If I can't have you, no one will."

Justin scrambled to his feet, his frustration mounting until he realized what was happening. Siffer had gotten to her. With each shot she fired, he wondered what was taking CPU so long.

Beverly suddenly turned. She looked right at him, right into his eyes. He hesitated. Had she seen him somehow? Then he sensed sudden movement within the shadows.

The shadows spoke to him, "Mr. Thyme, two can play your game."

It was Siffer.

Justin heard another shot, as searing pain radiated from his right thigh down into his foot. The impact knocked him to the ground. Beverly moved in closer and stood over him.

"She's not that bad a shot," Siffer said. He moved out of the shadows, into plain view. "She just needed my help to overcome your tricks."

Beverly stood, motionless, aiming the gun at Justin's head as he lay there. His wounds bled slowly, but his leg was worse. He put pressure on it with his right hand.

Siffer stood by Beverly's side. He looked down at Justin through sunglass-clad eyes. Justin squirmed in pain on the ground and Siffer slowly removed his sunglasses. Those red eyes burned into Justin's mind.

Justin closed his eyes and prayed.

"You've been a thorn in my side long enough," Siffer said. He looked at Beverly, stroked her hair, and then said, "Make this last shot count, my dear."

****

"Take a look at what Siffer's capable of, Derrick," CPU yelled as he typed one last set of commands. With his finger poised over the 'enter' key, he yelled, "Take that."

The security guard staggered suddenly. He dropped his nightstick and gripped his head, bellowing in anguish. The bright red in his eyes vanished and he fell to the floor.

Derrick was beside himself, "Did you see that? Did you see his eyes?"

"He was controlled by nanobots, stolen by Siffer from this very lab. Siffer modified them. He's poisoned Angel Falls and was using nanobots to get votes." CPU said.

Derrick eased up on the restraints and glared at CPU. "I told you, you're crazy," he said.

"You know it's true. Think about how you've been feeling lately. Can't place it exactly, but you haven't been yourself, right?"

"Just tired, stressed out."

"From what, too much free time? Remember that banquet you were at, the punch you drank?"

"You're trying to trick me," Derrick said.

"Think. Every time you start to have negative thoughts about Siffer, you get a searing pain in your skull."

"It-it hurts sometimes, yes."

"That's because you never trusted Siffer until after the banquet."

Derrick moaned in pain. "I think I...I passed out."

"The nanobots were taking over. I'll prove it to you."

Hoping for no more red-eyed interruptions, CPU switched to the program that would fix Derrick and everyone else. Then he connected his cell phone to the laptop. With a few clicks of the mouse, the program dial out.

"There." CPU looked up at Derrick, who looked sick, his face sweaty and flushed. "I'm done. When I hit this key, you'll all feel better."

He hit the 'enter' key, then waited for a sign.

****

Beverly poised the gun in both hands, taking final aim at Justin. Her hair, wet with sweat from nanobot fever, stuck to her face in clumps. The gun shook in her trembling hands. Suddenly she stumbled backward, the gun falling from her hand.

"Justin...?" she whispered, raising her hands to her temples. She fainted.

****

Seconds after the final keystroke, Derrick groaned and passed out. CPU rushed over to test his restraints. He then shook Derrick to see if he was back. It took very little to bring him around.

The first words out of his mouth were, "I'm hungry. What's to eat?"

"That's the Derrick I know," CPU laughed. He released the restraints.

Derrick sat up. "Where are we?"

"Don't you remember any of it?"

"I felt achy and my head hurt, but...hey, what's that?"

CPU heard it too, several moans and growls from beyond the lab doors. When CPU ran back to the laptop, several more windows had popped up. More figures with red dots were headed their way.

"Just a minute, Derrick. Once I take care of one last bit of business, we can get out of here."

This time, CPU left his cell phone connected. He quickly closed out all other programs, except the one that controlled the red dots. The program dialed out and CPU, with dramatic flair, punched 'enter'. "That should finish you all off,," he said.

Derrick looked on with growing confusion. "Finish what?"

"I'll explain later. Listen."

From beyond the lab doors, the sound of angry yells echoed through the halls, followed by the thuds of dropping bodies. Derrick bolted off the table as the last red-eye came crashing into the lab. His eyes instantly faded to normal as he collapsed to the floor.

Derrick looked cautiously at the body just inches from his feet. "Is he...dead?"

CPU closed up the laptop. "No, but we need to get out of here right now."

"You don't have to tell me twice!"

****

Siffer looked at Beverly. Realizing what had just happened, he let out a banshee shriek loud enough to wake the dead. Justin barely managed to get to his feet. The monument stood just a few yards away. He hobbled over to it as fast as the pain in his leg allowed and crouched down behind it.

An eerie red aura broke the blackness of the night and enveloped Siffer. He ripped the leather gloves from his hands, pulled his cape from his shoulders, and threw them angrily to the ground. Justin tried to become invisible.

"Do you think your simple tricks can stop me?" Siffer roared.

Justin sensed that his powers were no match against Siffer's. At most, he could only slow him down a little.

"Show yourself, like a man. Let's end this now," Siffer called into the darkness.

Something moved in the shadows to Siffer's left. He turned to concentrate his gaze in its direction. To Justin's horror, the man's eyes released a red flash that caught an unsuspecting groundhog dead-on. The animal squealed and burst into flames that consumed it within seconds.

"We are very much the same, you and I," Siffer said into the air, as he continued to search among the brush for Justin. "It's amazing how nanobots have enhanced both of our special genetic traits."

The nanobots were responsible for producing that much destructive electrical energy. Justin wondered why they didn't totally consume him - they were clearly destroying his mind. Fortunately, Siffer's eyes didn't seem to work as well as his own in the dark. His nanobots obviously had some limitations. The red glow they produced in his eyes might explain it.

"Of course," Siffer continued, "you are limited by an outdated prototype. I am indebted to GenEx Labs for supplying me with a newer model."

Justin tried to send his voice behind Siffer, off to his right. "We already know how you stole them—how you covered it up."

Siffer turned, briefly, toward the voice. He looked around, speaking slowly, deliberately, listening. "On the contrary, I've paid millions for them. Do you think my donations to GenEx were purely altruistic?"

Justin threw his voice in another direction this time. "You're finished. You don't control the voters anymore, everyone's been deactivated."

That hit a nerve.

"I'm finished?" Siffer growled. "Show yourself. We'll see who's finished." He thrashed furiously at the tall thicket and brush, searching.

"We know about Gordon and Senator Williams, it'll all be in the papers," Justin called from his dark hiding place.

Another nerve struck. Siffer's eyes flashed and burned the ground around him arbitrarily. He was getting closer. He was also getting careless.

"Weak fools. Only those fit for survival…"

Suddenly, he stopped. Justin heard it too: the sound of sirens approaching from far off. Too far to be of any help with Siffer almost on top of him.

There was no time left. He had to get out of there.

An intense blast caught the edge of the monument, just inches from Justin's face.

Scrambling blindly, Justin felt his way to the other side of the monument, when his hand landed on something metallic. His fingers closed around a grip of some sort. They fit perfectly.

He pulled. The object responded, slowly at first. Then, acquiescing to his touch, withdrew faster, glowing brightly and emitting a sharp, metallic ring.

His eyes slowly recovered from Siffer's blinding flash. He could see that he was holding the ancient sword in his hands.

Justin played with it, testing its awesome, perfectly balanced weight in his hands. It felt so natural. Each slice through the air rang out loudly. It handled with ease, in spite of his wounds.

But the sound had attracted another's attention.

A surprise blow sent Justin sailing backward through the air. He landed hard. He could feel Siffer's heavy footfalls rushing in for the kill.

Still clutching the sword with both hands, Justin raised himself up and brought the sword down hard to the ground in front of him. The earth split, opening a deep chasm that extended out to Siffer's feet, several yards away.

Siffer laughed sadistically as he, with a sideways somersault, rose into the air to land out of harm's way.

"You'll need to try a lot harder than that," he mocked. With a wave of his hand, Justin went flying again. He crashed into thorn bushes with such force that blood ran down his cheek.

Siffer was playing with him the way a cat plays with a mouse before pouncing on it. His own powers were useless against this pure evil. His strength was ebbing, his legs weak. The ground started to spin.

"I know your every weakness, Justin," Siffer shouted, as if reading his thoughts. "Before I finish you off, I will make you suffer."

He turned toward the edge of the plateau, to where Beverly still lay unconscious. He picked her up, cradled her in his arms and taunted, "How terrible it would be to watch helplessly as your friend is thrown over the falls."

The man's theatrics were infuriating. Justin angrily swung the sword around, pointed right at Siffer, yelling with everything he had.

"STOP!"

His voice, with tremendous force, sent harmonious vibrations down the sword's blade. The point glowed and vibrated. The sound grew in intensity. The tip burned white-hot with concentrated power when it suddenly exploded in a bolt of lightning.

It ripped into Siffer's side, throwing him, screaming, hundreds of feet from where he dropped Beverly. He slammed into an old oak tree, blackness oozing from his scorched side.

Seething with curses, Siffer got back to his feet. Electric sparks shot out across the overflowing blackness. Siffer covered his scorched side with one hand. The oozing temporarily stopped. Growling like an animal, teeth clenched, he hissed, "Time to finish this."

Justin watched in horror, as Siffer started to grow. He doubled in size. Yellow smoke belched from his nostrils and his eyes burned scarlet. He ran forward, but Justin stood his ground, holding the sword extended in front of him.

From several yards away, Siffer let out a thunderous shriek, which shook the ground. Justin lost his balance. Siffer flailed his left arm in Justin's direction sending a burst of energy that sent the younger man flying into a pile of rocks.

His bones were tough, but he was taking a severe pounding. He'd lost a lot of blood from the two gunshot wounds. The little strength he had left was quickly failing.

Another shriek from Siffer and Justin cried out in pain. Siffer's loud wails tore at the inside of his head. To alleviate some of the pain, he held the sword in one hand, covering one ear with the other.

Siffer ran at him, waved his arm again, pounding Justin into the monument. Again, another thrust of his hand threw Justin into the lake.

The cool water prevented Justin from passing out. He couldn't stand up as the weight of his wet clothes pulled his weakened body down.

Panic engulfed him: he'd dropped the sword in the lake.

Keeping his head above water, he madly felt around in the dark water. From the corner of his eye, Beverly moved in the distance. She was conscious. Siffer, bearing down on Justin, had forgotten about her until now.

Beverly was struggling, crawling with little success, as she tried to move away from the edge of the cliff.

She called out to him, unaware of his situation, "Justin, my leg...."

Justin was kneeling waist-high in the water when his groping hand found the hilt of the sword.

Siffer stopped short at the edge of the lake. He glared down on Justin. "I will take care of your friend; then, I will finally deal with you."

Siffer, with one bound, ran back to Beverly.

Summoning what remained of his strength, Justin tightened his grip on the sword. He summoned whatever angelic power he might have. He concentrated, focusing his mind on saving Beverly.

A Justin-shaped blur cut through the water. He was so fast the water did not have time to fill in the space where Justin had been, until he passed Siffer, finally reaching Beverly's side. His breathing grew labored and raspy from exertion.

At the edge of the precipice, he froze. The lights of the town blinked far below him.

Dizziness. Nausea.

The sword grew heavy in his hands. Beverly was so close, but so far. She seemed to be saying something to him, but only the heavy pounding of his heart filled his ears. He had to shut out the sight. He closed his eyes.

He heard her scream.

Siffer was now upon her, only yards from where Justin stood, frozen. Beverly, near the cliff's edge, was between Justin and Siffer.

"Say goodbye," Siffer snarled.

Siffer's face twisted into a menacing smile. His eyes widened, growing ever brighter.

Justin sprang forward, diving head first towards Beverly, the blade of his sword outstretched in from of him.

He sailed over Beverly, feeling the heat from Siffer's eyes. At that exact moment, a deadly flash from Siffer's eyes headed toward the young woman. Justin flew past her, the broad side of the sword receiving the full impact of Siffer's blast.

In an instant the blast, deflected off the blade, shot back to its source.

An unholy wail shattered the night; Siffer's screams echoed across the plateau. The human form engulfed by its own fierce heat and flames lit up the night. In seconds, the screams abruptly ceased, leaving a shadowy substance that floated and darted above the ground. Electricity arced upwards, shooting red sparks across the shadowy form as it hovered in front of Justin. It hummed, expanding and contracting as it became less cohesive.

A moment later, the form became silent and dark. It collapsed into billions of microscopic, dispersed particles on the ground.

Justin sat up and looked to his right. Another four inches and he would have joined Dawn at the bottom of the falls. Then he heard a moan from behind.

"You OK?" he asked Beverly.

"My leg's broken, but I'll be OK, thanks to you."

"Pretty view, huh?" Justin said with a grin. "My stomach hurts, but I'm cured of my fear of heights."

Beverly reached out her hand. "Just help me move away from here."

****

In all the excitement, Justin didn't notice the flashing lights. Finally, the police had arrived.

"Over here," an officer called. He was waving a plainclothes detective over to Beverly and Justin. Beverly recognized Tom.

"It's her leg, she needs a stretcher," Justin told the detective.

Tom eyed Justin cautiously. "You're not still going to use that thing, are you?"

The sword. Justin forgot he was still carrying the thing. He handed it to Tom, hilt first. "It saved our lives," he said.

"I know," Tom said. He took the sword, admiring its workmanship. "I saw the whole, unbelievable thing. How am I going to explain all this to the chief? What a mess. If that was Lou Siffer, I'd sure like to know what got into him."

"Nanobots. They fried his mind," Justin said.

"And the rest of him too, apparently," Tom quipped. "Let's get out of here. I'll have plenty of questions for you both, back at headquarters."

Chapter 23

Justin knocked before entering Beverly's office. Her leg was still in its cast. She greeted him with the warmest smile he'd ever seen. From behind his back, he produced a bouquet of carnations. He handed them to her and then took his usual seat across from her.

"I love these, but why?" She asked.

"I felt bad about your leg. How is it?"

"A little itchy, but mending. The cast will be off in two weeks."

Beverly picked up an empty thirty-two ounce soda cup she had left over from lunch. She hobbled out to the ladies room to fill it with water. When she returned, she placed the carnations in it, centering them on her desk.

"I'll find a nicer vase to put them in tonight," she said, taking a moment to admire them. She looked away. "I should be giving you flowers. I can't believe I shot you."

"You couldn't help it."

"Your arm healed amazingly fast. How's the leg?"

"The same." He smiled. "Must be another angelic trait."

Beverly started to say something before she hesitated, putting her hand over her mouth.

"What is it?" Justin asked.

"Dawn. I feel awful about her." Beverly said.

"She had some serious issues," Justin reminded her.

"I think she was actually Dr. Siffer's niece. I do know she was supposed to prevent you from interfering with his campaign plans."

Beverly's news revelation did not faze Justin. He had become well aware of Dawn's motives. That she was related to Siffer made sense. "She may even have tried to get me killed," he said.

"But," Beverly continued, "Consider how her treatment of you must have upset her. Look how it ended."

After a short, uncomfortable silence, she asked, "So, ready to get back to work?"

The question surprised him. "I thought my job ended with Siffer's demise."

Beverly leaned in closer, resting her arms on her desk. "Nonsense. You're the best thing that's happened to this paper in a long time."

Beverly may have been under the influence of nanobots, but some of the things she said on the plateau made Justin wonder. He hesitated, and then decided to ask anyway, "What about you?"

"What do you mean?"

"How have I worked out for you?"

Beverly actually blushed. "After what we've been through? How could you ask that? We're a terrific team."

"Oh." He decided not to probe her personal feelings further - for the time being. "So, I have a job. What next?"

She leaned back and smiled. "My promotion allows me to hire an assistant."

"I don't have any experience...."

"With your gifts, integrity, and talent you're the only one I want. You'll start by reporting on township and school board meetings. Bring your camera along, I love those photos. And, always keep your eyes and ears open."

Justin's eagerness quickly turned to caution. "Why? Are you expecting trouble?"

"I never want to be caught off-guard again, like I was with this campaign. You have a unique ability to detect and evaluate the unusual."

"Tom seemed impressed, too," Justin smiled. "Although, if he hadn't been there to see it..."

"We'd both be in a pickle," Beverly laughed.

"He doesn't know about me, does he?"

"No. And he won't. Not from me, anyway. It's best to keep that much just between us."

"And my friends. I didn't do this alone," he reminded her. "CPU saved my life."

Beverly reached across her desk for his hand. "And you both saved my life. I'll never forget it."

After spending several more minutes going over the new job requirements, Beverly accompanied Justin to her office door. She watched him walk down the hall and into the elevator. She smiled. They were a good team. And had become good friends, too. Very good friends....

****

When Justin responded to a knock at his door, he found Tom Selden was outside.

"Detective Selden, would you like to come in?" Justin asked.

"No thanks, Justin. I was just passing by and wanted to tell you that we have pretty much wrapped up the Siffer case. I also wanted to add that Angel Falls owes you a debt of gratitude. You're a very brave young man."

"Thanks," Justin said, a bit uncomfortable with the praise.

Tom pulled a small notepad from his shirt pocket and began scanning it as he spoke. "Siffer was slick, a nasty piece of work. That benefactor persona of his had us all fooled. We never thought to investigate him until that incident with you and

211

Beverly at the lake. I should have been more suspicious of Siffer when he protested a little too much over the stolen nanobots. He may have been a genius, but he was a poor actor.

"Siffer killed Mike Gordon over the missing security tape. It proved that Dawn had been complicit in stealing the nanobots. But get this: Siffer made the anonymous call that got Dawn arrested. His mind games really messed her up. No wonder she ended her life."

Justin, concerned about how much Tom Selden really knew about Siffer's powers asked, "What do you mean by 'mind games'?"

"Siffer was manipulative. He used people and threw them away. Heaven only knows what he had on Dawn. She was his niece for crying out loud."

"But why didn't Dawn's arrest backfire on Siffer? Wasn't he taking a chance by making that call?" Justin asked.

"Like I said, Lou Siffer exercised powerful control over a lot of folks. Maybe he shot Dawn up with nanobots – we'll never know, unfortunately. Siffer pushed her to commit suicide, which cleaned up another loose end – and any connection Dawn had with him.

"That senator who died, it was no accident. Siffer shot Roland Williams so full of nanobots his mind couldn't cope with the pressure. It literally blew up."

"I'm still tying up a few loose ends with this case and I may need to get some more information from you, Justin. This has been the oddest case I've ever handled."

****

Derrick, CPU, and Justin enjoyed an afternoon snack around the Thymes' kitchen table. A small TV on the kitchen counter aired a special news bulletin.

"...Many legal questions arise from the loss of Lou Siffer," the network anchor droned, "...a replacement candidate will be sought..."

"You sure can stir up trouble," Derrick chided Justin, his mouth full of chocolate chip cookies.

"You're not sore about losing your candidate, are you?" Justin shot back with a smirk.

Derrick threw a cookie at him in protest. "I told you all along that the guy was trouble!"

"It's just good to have you back to your old, obnoxious self," CPU said.

In what was considered an "unrelated story", the TV anchor reported on an "unprecedented number of fender benders across the state" from the night before. Miraculously, none of the accidents resulted in serious injuries. A whole host of unrelated mishaps had put people in hospitals, but again, none of them too serious.

"Didn't think of that," CPU said. "I'm glad nothing worse happened after we deactivated the nanobots."

Justin nodded. "More than one miracle got us through this week," he said.

CPU pushed his glasses up his nose. "I just hope we don't need any more miracles for a while."

Derrick patted CPU heartily on the back. "Not to fear, Justin's here. He's our very own miracle."

"No," Justin said, "he's right. We've been through a lot; it's time for a break."

Justin suddenly became quiet. These last few days proved he was here for a reason. Unfortunately, he couldn't shake the feeling that Angel Falls was in for more visitations - of the bizarre and possibly not-so-friendly kind.

His father had explained why he had been injected with the nanobots. Now, they merely functioned to enhance his endurance and memory. His other abilities were due solely to his emerging angelic nature, kept dormant all these years. It gave him extreme speed, the ability to pass through solid objects, and mind control.

Why had the nanobots remained in his system? Here was one mystery his father could not answer. If a symbiotic relationship could exist between the Nephilim gene and the nanobots, anything might be possible.

Anything.

Derrick thoughtfully munched on his eighth cookie, swallowed, and then looked over at Justin. "Nothing ever happened in this town until you got your wings." He smiled. Then he flinched when Justin kicked him under the table.

"Sorry about Dawn," CPU said.

Justin considered his few good times with Dawn. He weighed them against all the other things he'd discovered about her. It was better to have found out now, before he got too serious about her. How could someone who appeared so nice be so deviant? As for the authorities, they considered her case closed of suicide by drowning.

"I'm OK, CPU," he said. "I'm ready to move on."

"Into your new job at the Tribune," Derrick interrupted.

"Your editor - doesn't she know about you too?" CPU asked.

"Yes. She thinks we will work well together, my nose for trouble and all."

Justin relaxed into a daydream state. His thoughts turned to Beverly. Unlike his relationship with Dawn, he and Beverly went through a lot together, only to emerge on the other side stronger for it.

Beverly was nothing like her reputation, once you got to know her. He let his mind wander. In five or six years their age difference wouldn't be that important.

Yes, she certainly was becoming a very good friend.

Derrick poked Justin's arm, jolting him out of his reverie. "Hey! You having another vision?"

With a smile, Justin finished off the last cookie. "No. Just thinking."

The End

The author lives with his wife and children in rural Pennsylvania, just outside Pennsylvania Dutch country. He has five grandchildren, all boys. By trade, he is a computer technician.

CPSIA information can be obtained
at www.ICGtesting.com
Printed in the USA
LVHW010513090820
662601LV00007B/528

9 781949 472196